TRAUMA DRAMA

KAT PELUSO

TRAUMA DRAMA

Life in a State of Emergency

ARCHWAY
PUBLISHING

Archway Publishing books may be ordered through booksellers or by contacting:

Archway Publishing
1663 Liberty Drive
Bloomington, IN 47403
www.archwaypublishing.com
1 (888) 242-5904

ISBN: 978-1-4808-9221-7 (sc)
ISBN: 978-1-4808-9219-4 (hc)
ISBN: 978-1-4808-9220-0 (e)

Library of Congress Control Number: 2020914824

Print information available on the last page.

Archway Publishing rev. date: 09/17/2020

This book is dedicated to the outstanding emergency room staff members and the first responders that I was so privileged to know. These men and women put their lives at risk to save others. Not a day went by that I didn't learn something new.

I would like to give a special thanks to my daughter, son-in-law, and sister for their encouragement and support while I was writing this book.

PREFACE

THE LATE 1970s and the early 1980s were times of different social norms and many emerging social and medical issues. We were highly skilled, dedicated, and ever-so-young doctors and nurses who just wanted to make a difference. Some of us swore, some drank, and some just laughed. We used these coping skills as we managed and provided high-quality care in the most unimaginable, shocking, and difficult cases.

The stories set forth in the following pages are events and circumstances surrounding day-to-day life in a level-one trauma center. All names, characters, businesses, places, events, and incidents have been changed to protect identities.

1

I WAS HOPING that the emergency room would be uneventful today. It wasn't. *Shit!* I thought.

My name is Goldie Fisher BSN, RN. I am completing my first week of orientation in a major level-one trauma center. My previous ten years of experience was in the operating room and the surgical intensive care unit.

My preceptor is a twenty-nine-year-old registered nurse named Dave. He has had seven years of experience in this emergency room, and he has taught me much this week. This ER sees over two hundred patients per day. On this day, we are short a nurse, so I am left to fend for myself.

"Goldie, you cover these rooms and call me if you need me."

"Okay, Dave."

I nervously walk into room three, where a seven-year-old boy named Tommy has caught his penis in the zipper of his pants. As I enter the exam room, he is crying and clinging to his mother. She is also sobbing.

"Hi, Tommy. I'm Goldie. We're going to help you. Mrs. Johnson, Dr. Jason Metz will be in soon. Everything is going to be okay."

Dr. Metz is great to work with. He is focused and caring, not to mention incredibly handsome. He has had a long-standing relationship with his girlfriend, but this doesn't stop the nurses from hitting on him. Dr. Metz enters the room, introduces himself, and explains what he is going to do.

"No! No! No!" screams the little boy.

"Tommy, it's going to be okay. You'll be free in a couple of minutes." Dr. Metz uses a topical anesthetic and then manipulates the zipper.

"Noooooooooooo!" screams the writhing Tommy.

I firmly hold the boy and desperately try to comfort him and his mother. The doctor frees the penis of the frightened, wriggling, and screaming boy.

"Is he okay, doctor?" cries the mother as she hugs Tommy.

Dr. Metz smiles at Mrs. Johnson. "I assure you, there is no permanent damage." He leaves the room.

I clean the wound, and then Tommy stops crying. We have a little talk, and he promises to always wear underpants in the future—an all-important barrier between his penis and the teeth of an evil zipper. Discharge instructions are given to Mrs. Johnson. Goodbye hugs and a Popsicle are given to Tommy.

"Hey, Goldfish," Dave yells. *Goldfish* is his affectionate nickname for me. I affectionately give him the finger and follow him into trauma bay one.

"We are going to need your help in here," he says as the patient is wheeled in on a gurney. He looks to be in his twenties. "A car pulled into the ambulance bay, rolled this guy out onto the concrete driveway, and then sped off."

"Yikes!"

I am excited to work with such an awesome, well-coordinated team of doctors and nurses. We quickly wash our hands and don our gowns, gloves, face masks, and eye shields.

"Goldie, we are going to use spinal precautions. Cut off his clothes and do a head-to-toe assessment in sixty to ninety seconds." Dave hands me a pair of trauma shears to cut off the clothing. Oxygen is administered, IVs are started, and blood tests are drawn, which include a toxicology screen and an instant blood-sugar reading. The patient is placed on a cardiac monitor. His pupils are pinpoints, which could be indicative of a possible heroin overdose, so a reversal agent called Narcan is given to him. Radiology tests are ordered.

"I can't find any identification on this patient," I say.

"Chart him as John Doe."

As I am recording another set of vital signs on Mr. Doe, Dave says, "Goldfish, come over here."

"I'm on my way." I hear a commotion and look over my shoulder. John Doe has become combative. Several staff members are attempting to restrain him.

"They gave him more Narcan. This often happens

when we reverse their high with this drug, also known as naloxone. Dumbasses!" Dave winks at me.

"Incoming gunshot wound," Dave tells me after speaking with the triage nurse.

I hurry over to trauma bay four, wash my hands, and put on new personal protective wear. EMS wheels in the patient. He also looks to be in his early twenties. He is unshaven, shirtless, and covered with tattoos.

Another team quickly assesses him. He is agitated and restless, which makes it a challenge for the staff to hold him down in order to treat him.

Underneath the bloody dressing that EMS applied to control the bleeding, I see an entrance and an exit wound in his right shoulder.

"There is blood on the back of his jeans," states Dave. As we remove the jeans, Dave points out, "There is an entrance wound in the right buttock, but I see no exit wound." Dave carefully examines the jeans as he continues to cut them off. "We look for bullet holes in the clothing so that we don't cut through them. We have an obligation to protect forensic evidence. Goldfish, as part of your orientation, you will be scheduled for forensic training at the coroner's office."

"Wow, I can't wait. Dave, I see the gunshot wound in his butt, but I don't see any holes in his jeans. Oh shit, never mind. His pants were down." Dave gives me a big grin while we continue to care for the patient.

IVs are started and blood is drawn. He is sedated, is intubated, and is put on a cardiac monitor. Radiology tests are completed, wound care is done, and he is ready to be transferred to the operating room. I gaze toward bay one and see John Doe being wheeled out of the ER on his way to the intensive care unit. It looks like they have him in restraints.

Dave then escorts me over to the acute area, where he will assist with one cardiac arrest and I will assist with another.

"Which one do you want?"

"Is this a test?" I ask him.

He gives me the man stare.

I choose a sixty-year-old woman named Mary. I have been trained in advanced cardiac life support, and I have participated in many resuscitation situations.

I really enjoy working with Dr. Max Andrews and this medical team, as we attempt to revive Mary. As wild and crazy as this ER staff appears to be, I would welcome their care for me or anyone in my family.

What an adrenaline rush it is. It's pure organized chaos. That is why I transferred into the emergency room.

After thirty-five minutes of chest compressions, ventilation, and medications, Dr. Andrews asks, "Are any of you uncomfortable with stopping the resuscitation?"

No one objects. CPR is stopped, and he pronounces Mary dead. That nanosecond between life and death always fills me with awe. I feel like my mind slips into slow motion as life slips away.

My thoughts are interrupted by Dr. Andrews's voice. "Goldie, will you come with me to talk to the family?"

"Sure."

We then walk to a private area in the ER to meet with them. Mary's family looks terrified as we enter the room.

"I am Dr. Andrews, and this is Goldie Fisher." He tells

them of the resuscitation efforts and then says, "We did everything we could. I'm sorry, but Mary died."

"No! Please, God, no!" Mary's daughter cries out. The tears are streaming down her face.

Mary's sister falls to her knees and starts praying. Dr. Andrews leaves, but I take them to see Mary and support them in their grief.

My eyes well up with tears. I can't cry. Everyone knows that ER nurses don't cry. We are thought of as stoic, hard-core people who thrive on chaos. *Okay, Goldie*, I say to myself, *get a grip*.

When the family leaves, we prep Mary and send her to the morgue to await pickup by the family's chosen funeral home. I glance over at Dave, who has had a different outcome. They are transporting his patient to the coronary care unit.

Other patients are waiting, so I hurry to area three. As I round the corner, a fellow RN named Janet is disputing something with Dr. Georgius. She is looking up at him (He is very tall, and she is very short). Her face is flushed, and she hisses at him, "You can't yell at me, I have big tits!"

"Whoa, Janet, what can I do to help you?" I attempt to coax her aside. Much to my surprise, the doctor laughs loudly and walks away. "Janet, that is the medical director. Aren't you worried about sexual harassment?"

"Hell no! You have to have an unusual sense of humor if you want to work here and save your sanity," she replies and then laughs. "Don't you know that bizarre humor can relieve stress? Sometimes there is so much tragedy. This is how we cope. You'll soon learn."

I don't know what to say.

"By the way, you'll learn to swear a lot too. Some places offer comfort carts for bereavement. We have Southern Comfort carts located at the corner bar for the end of each shift. Join us. It really helps." She giggles and walks away.

I just shake my head and go to see a new patient in room nine. The patient is an eighty-six-year-old male who is having trouble urinating. He has intermittent confusion, but he is able to carry on a simple conversation.

"Hi, Mr. Morgan. I'm your nurse. My name is Goldie. I have to put a catheter into your bladder via your penis." I explain the procedure. "Do you have any questions?"

"No, just do it."

It takes patience and a few minutes to get the catheter to slip past a probable enlarged prostate. I then hook it up to a collection bag. I hand him the call light. "Mr. Morgan, push this button if you need anything. Please show me how you use the call light."

"Yes, push button," he says as he pushes it. I shut it off and leave the room.

I start a couple of IVs on new patients. Then I hear a man yelling, "Hey, where's the blond who was playing with my dick?"

I think, *Oh shit, is he calling me?* I grab Dave and ask him to go check on the gentleman in room nine. There is no way that I am going back into that room. I am on my way to teach someone to use crutches. After all, Dave did tell me that I had to function on my own today.

After giving aerosol treatments to a couple of asthmatic children, I go to room five to see a forty-nine-year-old male. He is well known to the ER. He is a homeless man named Melvin, who is also a frequent flier.

He slurs when he speaks. He tells us that he went to another hospital, but they put him in a cab and sent him to us. He is very drunk, and the staff is taking bets on how high his alcohol level is. I am listening to numbers that would kill you and me. Melvin is almost nonresponsive but easily aroused. IVs are started. It is cold outside at night, and he has no shoes but only some dirty socks on his feet.

"If I were you, Goldfish, I wouldn't remove those socks."

"Okay, Dave, I'll take your word on this one."

Melvin's alcohol level reads four times the legal limit. He is going to be here for several hours. Dave tells me that they always give him a box lunch when he sobers up and before he is discharged. I feel so sorry for Melvin. I have never been around patients like him. I slip a twenty-dollar bill into his pocket with a note that reads, "Buy shoes." Little do I know that this act of kindness would come back to haunt me the next day.

"Well, Goldfish, you did well being on your own so soon."

"Thanks, Dave."

"By the way, Goldie, tomorrow you will report to the coroner's office at 8 a.m. Ask for LeAnn. She will be expecting you and will begin your instruction on how to preserve evidence when dealing with trauma and sexual assault."

I smile at him, drag my sorry ass to my car, and head for home sweet home. I live on a forty-foot sailboat. I drive to the yacht club and walk down the dock. It is so relaxing here. It's almost like being on vacation. I climb aboard. I'm too tired to socialize, eat, check my mail, or watch television. I make a martini and get ready for bed. I just want to sleep.

I hear ambulance sirens. Oh, it's just my alarm clock. It's 5 a.m. I jump out of bed and get ready for another challenging day of who knows what. My first stop is the coroner's office promptly at 8 a.m.

I am so excited. LeAnn greets me and proceeds to show me around. We go to a conference room where I learn how to preserve evidence and to handle potential illegal substances, which I will remove from patients' clothing or body orifices.

"Body orifices, really?"

"Really," LeAnn says, chuckling. She then proceeds to teach me how to find and remove the alleged drugs and/or paraphernalia.

I am taught how to conduct an alleged-rape exam and to preserve the evidence. This is a very lengthy exam with complex procedures.

"Many of these cases will end up in court," states LeAnn. "Proper procedure, detailed, objective documentation, careful labeling, and security of the specimens are a must." Little do I know that I am being trained so that I can teach all the ER nurses sexual-assault protocols.

I learn how to cut off clothing while preserving evidence from gunshot and stab wounds. Lastly, I get to witness an autopsy that is underway before I leave to return to the emergency room. I have been at the coroner's office for six hours. What a great experience, but damn, I can't get the smell of formaldehyde out of my nose. I leave and head to the ER.

As I enter the emergency room, Dave can't wait to talk

to me about Melvin. He takes me to the conference room, looks me in the eyes, and states, "Melvin returned about four hours after he was discharged yesterday. He was as drunk as a skunk again. He had a note in his pocket that read 'Buy shoes,' but he had no money or shoes on his feet."

I look at Dave like I am a deer in the headlights. Damn! I then get a lecture on the behaviors of homeless drunks. I say nothing. I just stare wide-eyed at Dave. Finally, I have to vow that I will never enable another homeless drunk in the name of charity again.

"Well, Goldfish," Dave says, "we need to toughen you up a bit. Then I think you are going to fit right in." I feel like an *ass*!

2

WELL, I HAVE completed one week of orientation. Today I am working with Dave in triage. He says, "We assess and check in every patient. Then we prioritize the severity of their problems and the order in which the physicians will see them." I nod that I understand.

The first case is a seventy-two-year-old man in acute respiratory distress. He is working hard to breathe. He's wheezing—using his accessory muscles—and he can't talk in full sentences due to his shortness of breath.

"Why did you wait so long to come in?" I ask him.

He replies, "Lady," breath ... breath, "I call 991, and nobody come," breath ... breath.

"Oh dear, it's 911," I tell him. "Let's get you back to

room two and immediately get your breathing treatment started."

The next patient to be triaged is a nineteen-year-old male with a complaint of *abdominal* pain. He appears to be in no distress. "How long have you had this *abdominal* pain?" I ask him.

He tells me it has been a couple of days and then points to his belly. I ask him to rate his pain on a scale of one to ten, with ten being the worst pain imaginable. He responds, "Eleven," as he reaches into a bag that he is carrying. He pulls out some fast-food restaurant's French-fried potatoes and eats them.

"Okay, go sit down in the waiting room. Try not to eat any more French fries, and we will call you in a little while."

As he walks away, Dave quietly says, "Been here before. Poor excuse for drug seeking. Next patient."

It is getting busy. All of a sudden, there are ten patients lined up at the window, and two ambulances have just arrived. The first ambulance brings a child that has had a seizure. The mother is sent to registration. The paramedic tells us that mom said the child had a fever for four days and that she had no money to buy any medicine. The patient is unresponsive to verbal stimulation and is quickly triaged and taken to an exam room.

After registration, I escort the crying mom back to be with her child. Lena has already placed the patient on oxygen, started an IV, and drawn blood. As I turn to hurry back to triage, I hear Lena explaining the postictal state after a seizure and the treatment plan. Lena often appears to be a hard-ass RN, but here she is being so loving and caring to this mother and child. Social services will also assist in this case due to the inability to buy any medication. Back in triage, Dave continues to sign in patients. He tells me to take their name and chief complaint. Then I decide if they can go sit down in the waiting room or need to be taken immediately back to a treatment or trauma room.

Dave reaches under the desk. "There is a button under here. It's called a panic button. Press it if you ever feel in danger from a patient or family member."

"Wow, Dave, I hope I never have to use it." He then tells me where the other panic buttons are located throughout the ER. "We are a level one trauma center located in a high-crime area. Security responds very quickly when one of these buttons is pushed." Dave is relieved by a middle-aged RN named Carla and then goes to grab a bite to eat.

Carla has worked in this trauma center for twenty-some years. She is six feet tall and has a head of short, thick gray hair. She is stern, and she doesn't take any sass from anyone—patients, family members, or staff. "Go sit down and wait until you are called. Next," I hear her say.

A young, expressionless man appears at the triage window. He looks me in the eye and softly whispers, "Help me." I push the control to open the door and to let him into the triage area. His hand is at his side. In his hand, I see a huge knife—a machete. I freak out. I swear as I see my life flash before me.

Carla calmly presses the panic button. She stands up and very calmly and slowly says, "Put the knife down. Put the knife down. We want to help you, but first, you must put the knife down."

The man takes a step closer, and I feel my heart leap into my throat. Carla again says, "Sir, please put the knife down. Then sit here so we can help you!"

The ER's security guard is cautiously moving closer. The patient slowly begins to lower the machete as more security guards arrive. The ER's guard holds his hand up, signaling them to stop and hold their positions as he continues to ease closer. The patient then drops the machete.

I kick it toward the ER's guard, who immediately removes the weapon from our site. The other officers surround us and offer protection while Carla talks to the patient. He is shaking, but he lets me take his vital signs.

Security then escorts the man to a private area. One guard stays with him while he is seen by doctors and is admitted to the psychiatric unit. Security also removes the machete from the ER.

Whoa, now I can catch my breath. I look at Carla, and all I can say is, "Wow!" She grins at me and nonchalantly goes right back to triaging other folks. Dave was right. Security guards do come quickly.

Carla and I are told that we did a great job controlling the situation. I didn't tell them that I almost shit myself. Thank God for the panic buttons, the security guard, and awesome Carla. Dave sure picked a great time to leave and get something to eat.

Where is Dave? I hope he gets back soon. My thoughts are interrupted as a man runs into the ER via the ambulance bay, yelling, "My wife is having a baby in the car." At the same time, EMS is bringing in a possible stroke patient. I direct the paramedics to take the stroke patient strait to one of the critical-care rooms. The stroke team has been alerted, and it is waiting in the ER. From the onset of stroke symptoms, there is only a three-hour window to prevent brain damage by administering thrombolytic medication to dissolve clots. Time is brain.

"Goldie, take a cart out to the car, get the pregnant woman, and bring her inside," states Carla. "Also, take some gloves, just in case."

In case of what? I think as I follow the man to his car. Oy, it is worse than I thought. Where is that Dave? The woman is lying in the back seat with her legs spread-eagled, as she moans and pants. I count five other kids jumping around in the car. "Sir, gather up the children and remove them from the car *now* so I can help your wife."

I can see the baby's head crowning. I have no choice but to throw on the gloves and get ready to deliver the baby in the back seat of the car. Thank goodness, the father took the other kids to the waiting room.

"Push, push again," I tell the mother. She pushes and lets out a long scream. "It's coming. It's here. It's a baby girl."

Dave arrives just in time with some needed equipment. We clamp the cord and suction the baby's mouth and nose. The baby starts to cry. What a beautiful little sound.

"Can I see my baby? Is she okay?"

I smile and place the baby on Mom's stomach, and she hugs and holds her. We cover the mom and the baby with a sheet. A couple of paramedics assist us to get them on the gurney and into trauma bay three, which has been set up for deliveries.

The cord is cut, the newborn is crying, and the mother is talking to her new little girl. The labor and delivery team members arrive and take over. What a welcomed sight they are. They complete the birthing process. Mom gets to hold the baby for a few more minutes. Then the rest of the family is brought in to see Mom and the baby before they are transferred to the postpartum floor.

Dave and Carla tell me what a good job I did. I tell them that I am going to get a T-shirt made that reads, "I ain't birthin' no babies." They laugh. Delivering babies in the ER is my least favorite thing to do. Somehow, I am always the one who gets these patients. Go figure.

We get a call that the helicopter is bringing in a patient from a motorcycle accident. Carla stays in the triage area and continues to sign in ambulance and walk-in patients.

Dr. Mia Vaughn, one of our ER doctors, is on the flight. She gives us a brief report via the flight communication office to the ER and asks us to have the operating room and its staff members stand by. Dave and I go outside to meet the critical transport helicopter. Man, it really kicks up a wind when it lands.

Dr. Vaughn, Dana, who is an RN, and a medic deplane with a forty-five-year-old male patient who is on a backboard for spinal precautions. His neck is immobilized with a hard cervical collar.

Dr. Vaughn gives us the full report. "He was on a motorcycle and was struck by a pickup truck. He has a heartbeat but is unresponsive. He is intubated and receiving 100 percent oxygen. He has a normal sinus [heart] rhythm on the cardiac monitor. We inserted two IVs. One has fluids running in and the other has a norepinephrine drip to treat his low blood pressure. Both of his legs are splinted."

His face is swollen, bruised, and unrecognizable. He

is very bloody. Transfusions will be given during surgery. New vital signs are obtained. Dana hands me the patient's wallet, saying, "Here is his ID. The police got ahold of his family." A fast and thorough trauma workup is completed, and the patient is off to the operating room. Dr. Vaughn and the flight crew leave, and the police finish their reports. I return to triage.

I put through a patient with a sprained ankle, two patients with back pain, four people with lacerations that require suturing, two children with fevers, and a diabetic man. They are all routine and chief complaints.

Then in comes a young woman who sits down and whispers her chief complaint. "I have a mouse in my vajaba."

"Excuse me. Can you repeat that?"

"I have a mouse in my vajaba," she repeats and then points to her crotch.

"What makes you think you have a mouse in your vagina?"

She looks around then whispers, "I put my head down there, and it smells like a dead rat."

We get a lot of patients with infections and sexually transmitted diseases, but I have never heard anything described quite like this. I wonder which doctor I am going to give this patient to as I escort her to a chosen treatment room.

The patients just keep pouring in. They are all ages and have different diagnoses. Some are non-critical while others are extremely critical. Ninety-five people have come through in twelve hours. I'm looking forward to more shifts in triage.

3

I'VE BEEN GOING through two weeks of orientation. Today, I am to work primarily in the gynecological section of the ER. Lena is my preceptor this week. Our first case is a thirty-year-old, 375-pound woman whose chief complaint is abdominal pain and vaginal discharge.

Lena tells me, "When we assist with the pelvic exam, one of us may have to lean on or even sit on the head of the exam cart when we slide the patient down and put her legs up in the stirrups. This keeps the cart from tipping due to her weight primarily being on the lower half of the cart."

"Okay. Lena, will you handle the head of the cart? I'm not sure I'm comfortable with that yet."

"No problem."

Dr. Terry Berger enters the room and says, "Hello, Mrs.

West. I'm Dr. Berger, and I am going to perform your pelvic examination." He explains the procedure and then asks, "Do you have any questions before we start?"

"No."

"Mrs. West, I am Goldie, and this is Lena. We are going to assist with the exam. Let me help you slide down and get your legs up in the stirrups."

As I help her lift her legs, the doctor sits down on a stool at the foot of the cart. The patient shifts her weight, and the cart starts to tip. Lena, who has been holding the head of the cart down, is now sitting on the head of the cart, but son of a bitch, it's still tipping. The patient lifts her right leg off the stirrup as Dr. Berger frantically tries to keep her from sliding onto his face.

I run to the head of the cart, pulling the intercom cord on the way. When I add my weight to Lena's, the cart stops tipping. The secretary answers the call light, and Lena yells, "Send someone in stat."

Jeanette enters the room and helps reposition the patient as she reassures her that everything is okay. Poor Dr. Terry Berger wipes his face and then conducts the pelvic exam.

"Mrs. West, I am sending these specimens to the lab, and a nurse will phone you in two or three days regarding the results. I am also ordering you a prophylactic antibiotic today." Dr. Berger hurries out of the room. We pull the lady back up on the cart and tell her that we will be right back with her medication and discharge instructions. I leave and send the cultures to the lab.

"Where is Terry Berger?"

Lena looks at me, "He's probably puking and showering like he never has before." She laughs and walks away.

I think, *Oh, poor Dr. Terry Berger.*

I go into the next room. A twenty-one-year-old female injured her vagina last night, and it still hurts today. She is an exotic dancer. She placed two billiard balls in her vagina and pushed them out to entertain the crowd. However, she slipped, and the two balls clicked together and pinched the inside of her vagina.

Dr. Max Andrews comes in and does the pelvic exam. He assures her that she is fine but that she will be sore for a few days. He recommends that she doesn't put anything into her vagina for a week. He leaves the room with his hand on his forehead while shaking his head. Dr. Berger is still missing in action.

After Dr. Andrews has left the room, the patient looks at me and says, "I can't understand why I hurt down there a lot."

"Do you think it's because you shove pool balls up there? Perhaps I could better understand it if you used ping-pong or golf balls, but pool balls? They are huge. You may want to consider something smaller." I leave to go to the next room with my hand on my forehead while shaking my head. Dr. Andrews looks at me and laughs.

Oh good, Dr. Terry B. is back. A woman brings in her twelve-year-old daughter, who is having severe lower back pain. She is a tall, very obese twelve-year-old named Kayla.

"Mrs. King, has your daughter started having menstrual periods yet?"

"No, not yet."

The girl is writhing in pain and holding her lower back. Tears are streaming down her face as she says, "I hurt so bad."

Dr. Berger speaks with Ms. King and Kayla. "Based on her symptoms, I suspect that she may be passing a kidney stone, even at this young age. Goldie will get her into a hospital gown. We will give her something for the pain, obtain an X-ray, and see if she can give us a urine sample."

He leaves the room so that I can get her into a hospital gown. As I remove her jeans and panties, I see a baby's head crowning. Yikes! I hurriedly open the door and call to Dr. Berger. "Terry, come quickly. Your kidney stone has hair."

I ask the secretary to call a code pink to get the labor-and-delivery team here stat. I then help him deliver a baby boy. Margo, an RN, comes in to assist. She explains Kayla's situation to Mrs. West. The code-pink team arrives. They take over and prepare to admit Kayla and the baby.

Kayla is crying, and she looks confused. I think, *Fuck! This poor mother is in shock.*

"How can this be? I have never known Kayla to have a period. Oh my God, who did this? Son of a bitch!" She is swearing, crying, hugging Kayla, and kissing her new grandson.

I tell her, "Ms. King, we are going to the post-delivery floor and nursery now. A social worker will meet you on the unit and help you and your daughter understand and cope with the situation. She will assist you with getting answers to your questions while you bond with the baby."

The transport team arrives to take them from the ER to the admitting unit. Lena asks, "Damn, are you okay, Goldie?"

"Yes. This sucks. I can't imagine what must be going through their minds."

"Goldie, all we can do is hope they find the fucker who did this to a twelve-year-old and prevent him from doing it again."

After several routine patient exams, Lena explains, "The patients with vaginal discharge get a prophylaxis-antibiotic injection and then wait two days for their culture results. When cultures come back positive for a sexually transmitted disease [STD]), we call their homes and ask them to return to the ER. When they return for follow-up care, we inform them of the positive culture. We then ask that their partner or partners to come in for an exam and treatment of a probable STD.

"The woman who has never cheated on her man is now confronted with the fact that he most probably cheated on her, contracted the disease, and then passed it on to her. The patients' reactions vary: silence, crying, disbelief, and/or rage."

"I am sure that I will deal with this situation a lot."

"Unfortunately, you will."

Margo comes out of a treatment room laughing. She tells us that they just did a pelvic exam on a young woman. Dr. Berger informed the patient that he removed an object that looked like a condom. The patient smiled, clapped her hands, and yelled out, "Oh, that's where it went!"

"You should have seen the expression on Dr. Berger's face." She walks away still chuckling.

I go to see my next patient, who is a nineteen-year-old female and is complaining of vaginal discharge with a foul odor. Dr. Berger and I enter the room to do the pelvic exam. There is a horrendous, unpleasant odor in the room.

"Miss Jones, I am Dr. Berger. This is Nurse Goldie. We

are going to do a pelvic exam to find out what is going on. Do you have any questions?"

"No, please just fix me."

I position her and place her legs up in the stirrups. Dr. Berger inserts a speculum into her vagina and removes a soft secretion-covered object that reeks. I am trying to hold my breath and not to vomit while I double bag the specimen. Dr. Berger turns his back to the patient and gags.

"I am going to order antibiotics." He quickly leaves the room.

I assist Miss Jones back up on the cart and say, "I'll be back with your antibiotic." I can't wait to get out of that room and to get some fresh air.

After a few minutes, I stop gagging. I know I have to go back in that room. How can Miss Jones stand the odor? I try not to make her feel worse as I spray the room. "I'm so glad we got that out of you. Do you know what it is?"

"About a month ago, I rolled up paper towels to use as a tampon, and I guess I forgot to remove them. I couldn't afford to buy tampons. I'm so embarrassed."

"I am sorry you could not afford feminine products. In the future, a pad is a better alternative."

We admit her, and then we have the room disinfected. It's time for me to go home. By the way, Dr. Terry Berger resigned today. He'll be missed. I later learn that he moved to the west coast and bought a vineyard. There's nothing like wine therapy.

4

IT IS THE beginning of the fourth week of my orientation. I am not only in awe of the things that I see in the emergency room but am also curious as to what the first responders see and treat prior to bringing them to us. Some of our doctors have gone on runs in the ambulance. I wonder if it is possible for me to get this experience, so I speak with Dr. Georgius, who speaks with the head of nursing and the head of emergency medical services. I am permitted to ride with the squad as an observer during a day shift as part of my orientation.

I meet with paramedics Carl and Rudy. They orient me to the equipment in the ambulance, as well as go over their protocols. They emphasize checking the scene for safety.

"We not only go into homes and buildings but also

go to outside sites where there are car accidents, fights, shootings, etc."

"I will follow your directions," I say to Carl.

"Great! Here comes our first run. It is a seventy-two-year-old, unconscious woman."

Rudy drives, and I ride in the back of the squad with Carl. We arrive at the house.

The woman is lying unconscious, pulseless, and with agonal respirations on the living room floor. Rudy starts CPR, and Carl starts to apply the monitor/defibrillator.

The woman's son, who reeks of alcohol, grabs Rudy and tries to pull him away from his mother, yelling, "Stop hurting my mother!"

Carl motions me to stand back while he gets up and pulls the man away from Rudy, who immediately resumes CPR. Carl sits the man down and loudly explains that his mother's heart has stopped and that Rudy is trying to restart it. He calls for police backup. The woman is defibrillated twice and a pulse is obtained. Police arrive and keep the son under control. She is intubated, an IV is started, a sketchy history is obtained, and then a report is called in to the emergency room.

The police work with the man to find another family member to drive him to the hospital. It was shocking to see Rudy attacked while doing CPR and then Carl remove the man from Rudy.

"I feel very frustrated that I am to observe and not pitch in," I say to Carl.

"We need for you to be safe, and unfortunately, we run into this type of situation quite often," Carl says.

Off we go with the sirens blasting. The patient is

transferred into the emergency room, and the medics finish their report. The good news is that I don't have to deal with the drunken son when he arrives. My thoughts are interrupted by Rudy, who answers another call to go to a home where a twelve-year-old girl is having an asthma attack.

When we arrive at the house, the child is in respiratory distress. She is wheezing, using her accessory muscles, and speaking in one- and two-word sentences. Her name is Ann. She has a history of asthma, and she has had previous hospitalizations.

"Mrs. Lewis, has she used her inhaler?" asks Rudy.

"She hasn't had an inhaler for about three weeks because we can't afford it."

Mrs. Lewis and the house reek of cigarettes. Carl gives Ann two aerosol treatments.

"Mrs. Lewis, Ann needs to go to the ER for a possible admission. We will give her another treatment in route."

The mother rides in the front with Rudy, and Ann rides in the back with Carl and me while getting another treatment. I think, *Mrs. Lewis can buy cigarettes but can't afford her daughter's inhaler?* I am certain that a social worker will need to be involved in this case.

The patient is brought into the ER, and a report is given to Dave. He agrees that Sara the social worker needs to be involved.

"Goldie, how do you like riding with the squad?" Dave asks.

"It's really an eye-opener from pre-hospital to hospital. You never know what you are walking into."

"Looking forward to hearing all about it. Talk to you later."

"Later, Dave."

Carl approaches me and asks, "Are you ready to ride?" He tells me we are going to an apartment in a rough neighborhood. A man was beaten by his son, who took his money and his car. He was able to call 911 for help. The police should be there when we arrive and should have the scene secured.

We arrive, pull out the gurney and equipment, and then the police officers lead us into the apartment. Rudy is taking a history and conducting a physical examination. The man is in pain, and blood runs from his nose. His face and body are bruised. He is being placed in spinal precautions.

"Carl, what is that moving by the couch?"

Carl whispers in my ear, "Cockroaches. Look around."

"Oh my God! They are everywhere. What if they get on us?" I am freaking out while trying to look cool.

We continue to whisper so that the patient can't hear our conversation. "We will enter the ER through the hazmat entrance, get him into a hospital gown, and double bag his clothes."

"Yeah, but what about us?"

"We see this more than you can imagine. The rule is to never stand still but always keep moving. We will check ourselves. We certainly don't want to take any new pets home." He laughs. I start moving in place. He says, "If you are uncomfortable, you can shower and put on new scrubs. Double bag your old scrubs until you can wash and sanitize them."

We arrive at the ER and enter via the hazmat entrance. I feel so much better in my new set of scrubs.

"How do you guys do it?" They laugh and make scratching movements with their hands. "Very funny."

We grab a quick lunch. Carl says, "Come on, Goldie, we just got another call."

"This will be my last run with you guys today. How time flies."

"There was a report of screams coming from an abandoned building."

Several police are on scene, and they have entered the building to conduct a sweep. One of them motions us to hurry inside. We run in with our gurney and equipment.

"Oh my God!" There is a man hanging upside down from a rafter. He appears to have been tortured. There is saliva dripping from his mouth and blood dripping from the many cuts that cover his entire body—and I do mean his entire body. Everyone puts on rubber gloves.

"Quick, let's cut him down. Somehow, he is still alive!" shouts Carl.

They cut him loose and lower him onto the cart. He is suctioned, intubated, and put on oxygen with assisted breathing. An IV is inserted, and fluids are administered rapidly due to his extremely low blood pressure. A pressor medication is also started. The monitor shows a very slow pulse. Dressings are quickly applied to several cuts on his body. There is something tied around his waist. It is a cloth pouch with some weird symbols on it.

"Don't anyone touch that pouch. Let's just get him to the ER. Turn those sirens on and let's go," yells Rudy.

We race into the trauma bay. The staff members are

wearing their protective gear, and they take over while getting an updated report. We lift him onto the exam cart.

Dave asks, "What is that around his waist? I don't want to touch it. It's creeping me out. Maybe it's a voodoo thing."

"The cop said he looked like a victim of some kind of cult."

"Now I know I definitely don't want to touch it," Dave says as he assesses the man's multiple cuts. Carl is reciting something that sounds like an exorcism. Dr. Vaughn is making the sign of the cross as she cares for the patient.

"I heard that if, in your mind, you wrap yourself in silver, it will protect you from harm," I whisper.

We look at each other and say, "Done." After all, what do we have to lose?

Dave gets his trauma shears out to cut the line that is holding the pouch around the patient's waist. "I don't know what's in the pouch, but I hope it stays in the pouch," Dave whispers as he snips the line and the thing slides into a plastic bag. He quickly gives it to the police.

Additional IVs are started, and the patient's pulse and blood pressure are slowly improving. The man remains unresponsive. Blood is drawn, which includes typing and screening for transfusions, cultures, and toxins. This poor man is kept in spinal precautions as he gets an X-ray and a CAT scan. His right arm is splinted, and he is sent to the operating room, where they will deal with his cuts, fractures, and internal injuries. It is mind blowing that this man has survived.

I go to talk with Carl and Rudy. "Thank you both for taking me on your runs as an observer. In the ER, we care for patients who have come from unbelievable situations. What you see and do is amazing."

"Goldie, we never really know what we are walking into."

"Wow. The things you experience can be very scary and dangerous ... oh yeah, and itchy."

We have a good laugh, and they take off on another run. I watch them leave and get back to my reality in the emergency room. We are a little short staffed, so I volunteer to stay four more hours. Dave stays over as my preceptor.

Lena triages a delusional young female patient and puts her in room four. Mary Ann is a new nurse who transferred in from the ICU. She is standing at the medication-dispensing machine.

The patient in room four walks out into the hall and stands a few feet behind Mary Ann. She copies every move that Mary Ann makes. First, she pretends to put the pills on a tray. The patient then follows her toward room eight, walking with perfect, synchronized steps. When MaryAnn enters the room, the patient stops and waits. When she exits the room, the patient resumes mimicking her every move, even brushing back her hair.

We are trying not to laugh. MaryAnn is unaware of what is happening. I go up to the patient to convince her to return to room four. She tells me that she is the nurse and not the patient.

Dr. Vaughn helps me escort the patient to her room and calls for a psych consult. She then tells MaryAnn that she saw the woman following her and mocking her movements. Lena and Rachael are acting out the situation and giving MaryAnn a visual.

"Oh my gosh, I had no idea," states MaryAnn. We all chuckle.

Dr. Vaughn suggests that Mary Ann has no contact with this patient because this patient thinks she is Nurse Mary Ann. So MaryAnn works in triage with Lena. Lena calls back to the main desk, saying, "We are getting a seven-hundred-pound patient. Call the supervisor and tell her we need two bariatric beds stat." The hospital recently opened a bariatric unit, so the transporters are able to bring the beds to the ER quickly.

Two fire rescue teams pull into the ambulance bay. Todd, one of the medics, asks us to bring a bed out to the back of the squad. Maintenance has connected two bariatric beds and pushed the mattresses together to make one large bed to hold this patient. The patient is lying on the floor of the ambulance because the gurney wouldn't hold him. He is moaning and repeating that his belly hurts. It takes six people to transfer him onto the bed and then maneuver the bed into bay four.

Todd finishes his report. "His bedroom is on the first floor, but we had to cut through the wall to remove him from the house. The police are getting someone to board it up." We find out that the man likes to be called Ronny. He has a part-time home caregiver, who was not on duty yet. "Ronny was trying to urinate. He turned on his side in order to get the urinal to his penis using a rear approach. He couldn't reach his penis from the front over his belly." Todd then lists Ronny's medications.

We walk back over to bay four. Dave is attempting to obtain IV access. Dr. Metz is inserting an arterial line.

"Goldie, when we are done, we'll help you insert a

catheter so that we can monitor his urine output." They help me with the catheter's insertion by pushing up his rolls of fat so that I can reach his penis. I pray that they don't drop them on me while I insert the catheter and hook it up to a collection bag.

Ronny is too large for the CT scanner. Portable X-rays are obtained, and blood is drawn. He is medicated and ready to be admitted. Rob, Janet, Dana, MaryAnn, and a transporter push Ronnie to the Bariatric unit in his custom bed. They return to the floor somewhat out of breath and let us know that it was a difficult task.

Lena brings a patient, who is in police custody for theft, to room eight. When he was arrested for theft, he complained that his chest was hurting. Dana goes into his room to do a workup. He appears to be cooperating with her.

I hear Dana tell him, "I'll be back in a few minutes. I am going to get the supplies so we can start an IV and do an EKG." The patient asks her for a urinal before she exits. The cop steps outside the door to give him some privacy.

I continue walking down the hall when I hear a loud noise, and something or someone falls through the ceiling and almost lands on me. Dust and debris are everywhere. A man is lying in the middle of the debris, moaning, and holding his leg.

When Dana and the cop returned to room eight, the patient was gone, and they could see that a ceiling tile had been removed over the cart. The cop and Dana come running. Dana yells, "That's our man from room eight." Apparently, he tried to escape. He went about thirty feet before he fell through the hallway's ceiling.

Someone hits the panic button and security arrives. Fortunately, we get it under control. We get him on a backboard with spinal precautions and lift him up on the cart. The cop immediately handcuffs the patient to the cart. Dr. Metz examines the man. He is negative for a cardiac event. There are no injuries to his spine or neck. He only has multiple bruises and a fractured left leg. He is splinted, x-rayed, and admitted, after an orthopedic consult is obtained.

Dave comes up to me and asks, "Are you all right?"

"Yeah, he didn't land on me."

"Thank God. Nothing bad can happen to you on my watch." He chuckles and starts to walk away.

I follow Dave to room six. We're just about ready to release a seven-year-old girl who had a laceration on her forehead sutured. Dave is giving the mother discharge instructions, and I am getting little Tammy a Popsicle. Just as they leave, we hear an overhead page: "Code red, emergency room nine. Code red, emergency room nine."

"What? That's not a test alarm. It's real," I say.

"Come on, Goldie, let's go to nine."

Several staff members are running to room nine. The door is open.

Dave calls out, "I smell smoke."

Dr. Metz runs into the room with a fire extinguisher, which he took from a security guard. It looks like there is a burning sheet on the floor. Dr. Metz extinguishes the flames just as the firefighters arrive on scene.

A psych patient is lying on a cart in the room. He is in leather restraints and holding a lighter. He is laughing. Apparently, even though his arms were restrained, he managed to get his hand into his pocket, pull out a lighter, and ignite the sheet that had been loosely covering him. By some miracle, the draft from the fire pulled the sheet off the patient and onto the floor. The patient was not burned.

The patient is moved to room two, and a staff member is assigned to stay with the patient at all times. Incident and fire reports are made. The supervisor notifies all senior staff members that a meeting is planned for the following day to discuss the situation and to make plans for future prevention. Environmental services cleans up room nine.

"Goldie, our overtime is up. Let's get out of here. I need some sleep," Dave says.

"Me too." I tell Dave. "My day was surreal. Just give me the bag with my scrubs from the cockroach house."

He gets my bag of scrubs. I throw them in the big garbage can on the way out the door. It's time to head home for some well-earned peace and quiet.

5

WELL IT'S WEEK five, and I am in my last two weeks of orientation. I am on the night shift, which is 7 p.m. to 7:30 a.m.

During my interview for the ER nurse position, the vice president of nursing, Karen Johns, told me that the night shift is where I'll see the most trauma. I clearly remember her. She said, "Goldie, it will make or break you as an ER nurse. I'm betting it will make you." Karen is always supportive and a great mentor.

I will be working closely with Dr. Jason Metz, Dr. Mae Vaughn, Dr. Max Andrews, Dr. Myron Baum, and RNs Tina, Janet, Rob, and Janette. We waste no time getting started.

In comes EMS with an eighteen-year-old male with a

gunshot wound to his right hip. Janette and I swiftly cut his clothes off, being careful to protect any bullet holes in his clothing. His name is Duane. He has four pagers on him, and one of them is beeping.

I naively and stupidly ask, "Why do you carry all of these pagers?"

"I'm a beeper salesman, bitch."

Janette laughs and whispers in my ear, "Drugs."

Well okay then, moving right along, Dr. Myron Baum (He likes to be called Myron) is a third-year resident doctor. He orders a CAT scan. Myron and I wheel our patient into radiology. I assist by sliding the patient onto the scanner table. The scan is completed. As we slide him back on the gurney, I see something that looks like a piece of plastic stuck to his buttock.

I whisper, "Myron, do you see something on his butt?"

"Yes, I do."

We carefully roll Duane just enough for Myron to pull the remaining plastic, which is a baggie, out of his rectum. Duane shouts, "Get away from me, you fuckers!"

The radiology technician pushes Duane back down on the gurney. The baggie is filled with a white, powdery substance.

Myron and I look at each other. "What do we do now? Put it with his belongings, throw it away, give it to the police, or snort it? Just kidding!" the radiology tech says and then laughs.

The patient yells, "Put it with my clothes or throw it away."

"Is that cocaine?"

"None of your fuckin' business, you fuckin' blond bitch."

Myron is holding the baggie. He looks at the patient and says, "We will turn it over to the police in the vehicle that came in behind the ambulance that brought you here." Duane spits at Myron, but luckily, it misses him and lands on the floor.

The cops are not happy about the hidden bag of white powder. Now they have to write another stinking report on this guy. I wonder, *Is there no end to this madness?*

Paramedics bring in a twenty-three-year-old male who was beaten with a baseball bat outside of a nightclub. He is unconscious, and his face is covered with blood. He is intubated and being manually ventilated with a bag-mask device.

As we begin to remove his spandex pants, Rob points and whispers, "Look at that large bulge in his pants." Rob continues cutting off the pants and asks, "Is anyone hungry?"

"What?" asks Dr. Vaughn. Lo and behold, the patient has some kind of sausage taped to his inner thigh. "I think I know why someone beat him," says Rob, chuckling. Off he goes with Rob and Dr. Vaughn to get a CAT scan.

The police officers come in to finish their report. I inform them that the patient is having a scan. I particularly like the police officer named Billy. He is originally from California, and he wears steel-toed boat shoes with his uniform. He is in his late forties and is an avid sailor (as am I). He has a fantastic fifty-foot sailboat. We briefly share adventures that we have had at sea. Billy is a family man, cop, sailor, and all-around nice guy.

Now I'm on to my next patient. Tina, the youngest nurse in the ER, asks me to assist with a forty-nine-year-old female from a motor-vehicle accident. The patient is unconscious and immobilized on a backboard. She has a hard cervical collar around her neck. She is intubated with assisted ventilation and 100 percent oxygen.

Her face has been partially degloved. Her peeled-off face is bloody and hanging like something from a horror film. Her right leg has been amputated below the knee. Paramedics have wrapped the severed limb in plastic, and they set it in a basin of ice. The stump has a tourniquet around it with several pressure dressings. Her right arm is splinted.

George, the paramedic giving report, tells us, "We had to cut off the top of the car to extricate her. Her head had gone through the windshield, and her face had degloved as her head repelled back inside the car. The engine motor had pinned her legs and severed the right one. The scene was a bloody mess."

"I can only imagine what you guys see at the scenes. You are amazing." I start to insert an additional IV line as Dr. Vaughn keeps shouting out orders. Tina moves swiftly and gets them done. There's so much blood.

All of a sudden, a car crashes through the wall of the trauma bay. It just misses hitting Dr. Vaughn and Mandy, the respiratory therapist. Debris is flying through the air.

"What the fuck?" I blurt out.

The staff is screaming, swearing, shaking, and I think I peed myself a little. I hit the panic button. Tina, Dr. Vaughn, and I continue caring for our trauma victim.

Dr. Andrews, Rob, Dana, George, another EMT, and the security guard approach the car.

More help arrives. Dr. Andrews and the EMTs pull the driver out of the car while protecting his neck and spine until he is immobilized. Rob, Dana, and our security guard pull the second person out of the back seat, who appears to be having a seizure.

Other police officers have arrived, and they attempt to get a report from the driver. Apparently, the driver was bringing his buddy, who was seizing, to the ER. He drove into the ambulance bay and hit the gas instead of the brake. The rest is history. Thank goodness, no staff was injured or killed. Both the driver and his buddy are treated and admitted. The car is towed, and the wall is being temporally closed up by maintenance.

In the midst of this chaos, we get our accident victim to the operating room. Several teams are assembled to reattach her face, reset her arm, and transfuse her. They will possibly be able to get her severed leg reattached.

Just as I am on my way to the restroom, a police officer runs in from the ambulance bay. Tears are streaming down his face, and he is carrying a German shepherd that has been shot. "Please help him. Help him!" he yells and then runs to the trauma bay. Myron and I follow him.

Myron stammers, "I-I can't. It's a dog."

"It's no dog. He's my partner. Please help him." Tears continue to pour from his eyes (mine too).

Dr. Metz runs over and assists Myron (Dr. Baum). Dr. Metz is adamant. "We will help him. Put him in trauma bay two and hold him tightly." Dr. Metz instructs me to get pain and sedation medications. "What's his name?"

"Buddy, his name is Buddy."

Dr. Baum sedates Buddy. Dr. Metz intubates the dog, administers oxygen, and supports his breathing. Mandy, our chief respiratory therapist, teaches the cop how to ventilate Buddy with oxygen attached to a bag, which he must squeeze every five seconds. Dr. Baum and I clean the area of the gunshot wound and apply a pressure dressing to keep the bleeding controlled. Tina calls an emergency veterinary clinic. We give a report and prepare to transfer our little patient, Buddy.

Two more police officers arrive and drive the cop and his wounded partner to the emergency vet clinic. The cop bags the German shepherd with portable oxygen all the way there.

Later in the shift, the cops return the oxygen tank. They tell us that thanks to our help, Buddy survived. Cheers go up in the ER.

We were later reprimanded for taking care of a dog, but if any police officer should ever bring in a wounded partner in the future, we will probably do the same thing. It did not impact the care of other patients. We took an oath to save lives—all lives. I have a feeling that my boss, Karen Johns, would have done the same thing. I swear I saw her smile and wink at me as I left the disciplinary meeting. I hope I grow up to be just like her. Now, where is that bathroom?

It's 3 a.m. EMS is on the way with a twenty-five-year-old male who is in cardiac arrest. As they arrive, CPR is in progress.

The patient's male friend disembarks from the ambulance. He is dressed only in a pair of shorts. He is loudly sobbing, hitting his head, and yelling, "I killed him. I didn't mean to do it!"

With some difficulty, our security guard and I take him aside to a private area and try to calm him down. I look into his eyes and ask, "What is your name? What happened? Please talk to me. What happened?"

The security guard is paged, and he leaves the room. Janet comes in to help me. Again, I say, "You have got to tell us what happened."

The man's voice is trembling as he speaks. "We were shrimping ... and ... and ..." He begins to sob uncontrollably again. I hand him tissues.

Janet whispers, "What the hell is shrimping?"

I look into the young man's face. "I don't understand, what do you mean by shrimping? Please tell us what happened."

He stands up, starts banging his head on the wall, and says, "I killed my love. I didn't mean for it to happen." He drops to his knees.

Janet hits the panic button to summon more help before he really hurts himself, or worse, he hurts us. Two EMTs and a security guard arrive and lift the young man up onto a gurney.

Dr. Andrews enters and says, "Is your name Jason?"

"Yes," he says, sobbing.

"I am Dr. Andrews. We did everything we could to restart his heart, but I am sorry to inform you that Bruce died a few minutes ago."

The young man, whom I now know as Jason, begins to scream. He jumps off the gurney and starts hitting his head with his fists. "I want to die too. I'm sorry, Bruce. I'm sorry!"

Dr. Andrews gives Janet an order to medicate Jason and then says, "Goldie, take him to a treatment room, put him on suicide precautions, call a psych consult, and prepare to have him admitted. The police officers on this case have both men's identifications, and they will give the information to the admitting clerk."

The medication is starting to calm Jason down. An ER tech stays in the room to observe him.

I talk to Carl, who is one of the medics that brought them in. I say, "He tried to tell me what happened. He said he was shrimping. What the hell does that mean?"

Carl then proceeds to tell me, "Shrimping is the act of performing anal intercourse. When the man ejaculates, he inserts a straw into the other man's rectum and sucks out his semen. Unfortunately, this guy blew a fart, and his partner sucked up a bolus of methane gas through the straw, which immediately put him into cardio/pulmonary arrest."

"Yikes! I never heard of such a thing. Son of a bitch, no wonder he thinks he killed his partner." Carl just shakes his head, shrugs his shoulders, and walks away. Trauma! Drama! Life in a state of emergency. When will it end? Is there a full moon out? It is known that ERs get extra crazy during a full moon.

I care for two more patients, who unsuccessfully attempted suicide. I perform CPR once more and tend to a patient with a superficial gunshot wound. I treat two diabetic patients and three asthmatics. I assist with resetting a dislocated right shoulder. After starting an IV on an infant, I drink a cola, eat a candy bar, and then give report on my patients to the oncoming shift nurse.

I am ready to leave the ER. It feels like I am in a MASH unit in a war zone. My head is spinning. Since our corner bar is not open at 7:30 a.m., Rob, Janet, Max, Mae, and I decide to go to the yacht club.

We sit on my boat, talk about the cases we dealt with, and drink Bloody Marys until 11 a.m. (as if we didn't see enough blood last night). We examine the night's events and the way we dealt with them. This helps relieve stress as well as sharpen our skills for the future. Eventually, everyone goes home, with the exception of two people who passed out in one of the cabins. I won't mention who or why. Let them sleep. It is almost the weekend.

I really enjoy my weekends off. After my divorce, I bought a forty-foot sailboat, which has become my home. I am so happy. Rob, Janet, Mae, and Max join me for a sail. It is a gorgeous Sunday. There are ten knots of winds and two feet or less of waves. It is smooth sailing. We have lots of food and drinks and soak up some sun.

We pass Police Officer Billy. He waves as he passes us. Damn, I love his fifty-foot sailboat.

"Nice boat," yells Rob. We all wave.

"Wow, what an impressive yacht. Too bad he's married," states Mae.

I agree, but Max frowns and says, "A big boat's not everything." Mae and I laugh. I think Max has the hots for Mae, and he would be quite a catch.

Rob and Janet go below into the galley to make some more drinks. They are gone for quite a while. Max goes below. He comes back up laughing and says, "Guess what

I heard going on behind a closed door?" He chuckles. "I'm not going to knock."

"Me neither," Mae and I reply.

Eventually, they surface with smiles from ear to ear and cocktails in hand. It turns out that this will not be the last time something like this happens on my boat. We all work hard and play hard. But I think, *I better never find "boy butter" on my cabin sheets.*

I sail back to my dock. While hooking up the power cords to the dock's power column, I notice an incredible fifty-foot sailboat pulling up to a dock across from mine.

I hear Mae say, "Wow, look at that captain. What a hunk."

Janet whistles, and I can't take my eyes off him or his boat. I snidely remark, "Girls, keep away from him. He's mine."

Rob and Max are not amused. Max states, "Maybe he's married or gay." I just give him the girl stare.

The guys make martinis while we girls make dinner on the boat. The rest of the evening is fun and relaxing. My friend Jim meets us at the cabana. He has a great sense of humor and keeps everyone laughing. After a swim in the pool and cocktails in the hot tub, a live band plays Reggae music, and everyone dances poolside.

Mae looks at me and says, "Goldie, this is a wonderful way to live. I feel like I am on vacation."

Max raises his glass and says, "Here, Here!" and we toast to more great sails together.

When they leave, I gaze over toward that gorgeous man on his fabulous sailboat. His crew appears to consist of two men and one woman. They are sitting in the cockpit, sipping drinks. *Hmm, I wonder who that woman is?* I think. Five a.m. comes fast, so I get ready for bed. I have no dreams of sirens and patients tonight but only dreams about me with a six-foot-five-inch naked man, with a perfect V-shaped back, tight buns, long legs, and the face of a movie star sailing on an awesome yacht.

6

I HEAR THE alarm clock. Damn, it's 5 a.m. already. I shower, don my scrubs, eat a light breakfast, brush my teeth, and climb off my boat and onto the dock. It's 6:15 a.m. I see Handsome sitting in his cockpit, drinking from a coffee mug. As I walk down the dock, he waves. There is no one else around but me, so I wave back. Okay, that's a start. I get into my car and drive to work.

It's good to be back on days this week. The night shift was wild. I saw and learned things that I never could have imagined. As I round a corner in the hospital, there is a man shouting at a female resident, who is consulting him on his mother. He is right up in her face. His mother weighs five-hundred-plus pounds. A bariatric bed has been delivered to the ER for her safety and comfort (The usual ER carts only support up to four hundred pounds).

The doctor tells him that his mother is very ill. "She is intubated and will be on a ventilator to help her breathe. We will admit her to the medical intensive care unit for monitoring and treatment."

The son verbally threatens the doctor, saying, "I will kill you if anything happens to my mother."

Two security guards remove him from the area. He yells all the way out of the ER while pointing his finger at her. As they pass me, he makes eye contact and yells, "You fucking blond bitch, you better not let anything happen to her either!"

The resident physician writes orders on his mother's chart. I care for this patient, along with several other patients, until a bed space becomes available in the MICU. We finally get an open bed. A respiratory therapist, a transporter, and I push her up to MICU in her bariatric bed. I am glad her name-calling son is not here. I still can't believe how many times I have been called variations of a fucking bitch. All have been totally unprovoked (I'm beginning to think that's my name).

I return to the ER. I care for two patients with chest pain and assist with three other patients being sutured. While at the nurse's station and obtaining discharge instructions for a patient, I suddenly hear a terrible ruckus. A man leaps over the counter, grabs me, and then spins me around. I look into his face. *Oh no, it's him!* I think.

"What have you done with my mother?" he screams as he starts to shake me. I am a black belt in defensive martial arts and use a technique to free myself from his grip. Two staff members assist me to contain him while security quickly arrives. Someone from the staff pushed that wonderful panic button when the man grabbed me.

I try to tell the man that his mother is in the MICU getting one-on-one care. The police arrive and intervene. They cuff him and move him into the police room.

I hear Dave say, "Good move you made, Goldfish. I didn't know you were trained in martial arts." He gives me a hug.

Dr. Andrews insists that I get checked out, even though I assure him that I am okay. I'm just shaken up. My examination checks out, and I complete the required incident report. I tell the police officers that I don't plan on pressing charges and ask them to escort the man to the MICU so that he can see his mother before they remove him from the hospital. They agree. Now I get back to work.

A mother brings in her five male children. They have had the sniffles, sore throats, and fevers for the last couple of days. The children's names are Moses A., Moses B., Moses C., Moses D., and Moses E.

I am curious and say, "Their names are unusual. I have not heard them before."

"When I want them all to come, I just have to yell Moses come here. Then if I only want one of them, I call him by his letter."

"I see," I say and then line them up alphabetically and obtain throat cultures.

Because of my own personal trauma that morning, the staff seems to give me a lighter load. I assist with applying casts on broken limbs and teaching patients how to ambulate with crutches, canes, and walkers. I care for two patients with myocardial infarctions. I transfer one of them to the cardiac catheterization lab. I start the other on thrombolytic therapy for blood clots. The shift will end soon.

What a day I have had. At the end of my shift, I am invited to be a Hobag (a group made up of the best emergency RNs). They handle the most difficult cases and are often subject to being called fucking bitches, hoes (ho stands for whore), or other scornfully abusive remarks by patients. There is only one honorary physician in the group: our beloved Dr. Andrews.

"I feel so honored you invited me to join," I say. They bestow upon me a polo shirt and a baseball cap with "Hobag" embroidered on them.

"You are now officially a Hobag," they shout out as they give me hugs.

Dr. Andrew hugs me and says, "Goldie, you are now one of the best. We help each other handle anything." I thank them again, and instead of the corner bar, I invite them to the yacht club for a celebration.

As we gather at a poolside table and order drinks, I see Handsome sitting at the cabana bar. He appears to be alone. I walk up and introduce myself. After all, I am the yacht club's commodore.

He stands up and says, "Hello, I'm Andrew Piers. You can call me Drew." We shake hands.

I say, "We saw you sail in. That's an incredible vessel. Welcome to the yacht club. Please join us."

We walk over to the poolside table, make introductions, and share information about ourselves. He owns his own business, and he can work from his boat as he sails to new destinations. He hasn't mentioned a wife or partner. Drew invites all eight of us to go for a sunset sail. What a great way to celebrate my becoming a Hobag.

Everyone is excited. I think that this could be the start of a fabulous friendship. Drew takes us on a tour of his boat.

"Wow, what a sailboat!" Max shouts. Everyone agrees with him. "Gee, I hope my boat grows up to look like this one." Drew laughs.

I release the lines as he backs out of the dock. Drew explains the rigging to Max and Lena. They nicely hoist the sails.

"Janette, do you remember where the bar and refrigerator are?" Drew asks. "Sure, I do, and I make wicked drinks. Come on Janet and Tina, you can help me." It is a perfect evening with martinis and a spectacular sunset.

"Goldie, do you want to take the helm?"

"Oh yes." I sail back to the dock while he helps the Hobags take in the sails and handle the dock lines.

We thank him, and as we depart, he gives me a kiss on my forehead. "Goldie, you have to sail with me more often."

"I would love to," I say. Then I think, *What is this teenage tickle in my groin?*

We all say goodnight, and they leave for their homes. I climb aboard my boat and get ready for bed.

At sunset, I sail. At sunrise, I work. As I drive to the hospital, I think about why I like the ER. Besides the rush of adrenaline, I like it because there is no sacred, professional hierarchy. Doctors and nurses call each other by their first names. They work and play hard together. These men and women are special and are very gifted in the field of medicine. They often work under very stressful conditions and may even appear wild at times. I feel very privileged to be a part of all of this.

As I enter the emergency room and get report from the RN going off shift, EMS rolls in and goes directly to the trauma bay. They bring in a middle-aged man who tried to commit suicide. Off go my rose-colored glasses, and I'm back to reality.

"What happened?" I ask.

A medic states, "This guy swallowed gasoline and then stabbed himself in the gut." A member of the squad keeps the knife secured in place. It is sticking out of his abdomen through thick bloody dressings.

Dr. Jason Metz has us call and alert the operating room to get ready for this patient. "We need to intubate this guy before we send him to the OR." As the doctor slides a tube into the patient's throat, I wonder if the gasoline burned his esophagus when he swallowed it. But we are working so fast, I don't have a moment to inquire.

The rest of us achieve additional IV access, draw blood to include a toxicology screen, and hurriedly transport the patient to the OR while manually bagging him with high-flow oxygen. We didn't remove the knife because that could cause more damage on the way out. It is much safer to remove it in surgery.

The staff members of the OR meet us at the door. "We'll take him from here."

"Okay, please leave our cart and equipment outside your entrance. We will pick it up before the end of shift."

They nod and disappear into the OR, and we hastily return to the ER.

Tina, Janette, and I care for several major medical, pediatric, and orthopedic patients. I think, *Damn, it's so busy. No time to pee or eat. We just get used to it.*

Five hours have passed, and Jason Metz receives a call from the OR. It is the surgeon who operated on the suicide patient. "What? No shit! Thank God, no one was injured," Jason says, hangs up, and calls us to the nurses' station. "They opened up the patient and removed the knife. When they proceeded to cauterize a bleeding vessel, flames shot up out of the incision like flash flames on a grill. Then the flames quickly extinguished themselves."

We are speechless. Residual gasoline and/or fumes in the gut—who would have thought this? It is a miracle that no one suffered any burns and that the patient survived.

I have been told that we receive more trauma patients than the designated county trauma center. I would like to think that it's because we are superior. Maybe it's because Rachael Jones, who is an RN, started cooking for the medics almost every shift she works. They get chili, hot dogs, mac and cheese, spaghetti, etc. The aroma flows out of the medic's report room. How yummy it smells. It also helps us when we need to grab a bite on the run because we rarely have time to take a real lunch break.

Just as I am about to enjoy one of those hot dogs, EMS rolls into the pediatric trauma bay with a five-year-old who sustained a gunshot wound to his head. CPR is in progress. Max Andrews runs the code. An intraosseous IV is started in the patient's right leg. The needle is driven through the proximal tibia bone and into the bone marrow.

This is a quick IV access during CPR. Medications are administered, and CPR remains in progress.

We continue CPR, even though we know our efforts are futile and as we observe blood and brain gray matter oozing from the exit wound. "He's only five fucking years old!" bellows Dr. Andrews. After forty minutes, he stops the code and pronounces the child dead. It seems surreal and so wrong to see this lifeless child before me. "Goldie, come with me to talk to the mother."

"Sure Doc." *Damn, why ask me, Max?* I think. I am trying desperately not to cry.

Mrs. Washington has been waiting in a private area. Our social worker, Sara, has been supporting her. The mother wails when she is told, "Despite all of our efforts, Leroy died a few minutes ago."

"Why, God? Why? My innocent little boy!" She drops to her knees and raises her hands skyward. I kneel down beside her and take hold of one of her hands. My eyes well up with tears. I think, *Damn, my mascara is smearing.*

Between the sobs, she talks to me. "There is often gunfire heard in our neighborhood—drugs and gangs! We usually lay on the floor when we hear gunshots. I never thought it would hurt us." She cries harder. I now am holding both of her hands as she continues to unload her emotions. "My baby got caught in the cross fire. That motherfucking scum don't care. To them, my baby is just a mushroom!"

We listen, and then I ask her if she wants to see Leroy. She is shaking, but she nods yes. We take her to Tina, who then escorts her to be with her dead little boy. Sara is asked to call the family to come into the hospital.

I talk to the police officer as he is writing his report. He reiterates what the mother told me. "Children shot in the line of fire are called mushrooms, and there is no remorse from the shooters."

"How horrific!"

"We have to secure the scene to protect the paramedics when they go to care for the wounded."

"What you first responders do sounds so dangerous." He smiles.

I go back and help ready little Leroy before the rest of the family arrives. As family members trickle in, they wail and pray. Tina and I keep trying to hold back the tears. *Remember, we are tough ER nurses. We don't cry, right?* I think.

The family remains for about an hour. Mrs. Washington leaves with them, tightly holding Sara's business card. Tina transports little Leroy to the morgue. I leave to find a mirror so that I can fix my smeared mascara. Then it's on to the next case.

The shift is over. Most of us decide to meet at the corner bar for a drink and to discuss the shift's events. Leroy's family was provided with a comfort cart. Now it's time for our Southern Comfort cart.

7

WELL, I AM back on the night shift. There are so many gangs, and they are so deadly. Young men are dying. The police department gives us information on various gang tattoos, graffiti, language, and some initiation practices. The police department wants to be notified if we receive any trauma patients whose injuries appear to be gang related and have not been escorted to the ER by police officers.

Lately, we have seen a run of teenage males with bullets through their right feet but none through their right shoes. We are informed that this is a gang initiation. We care for their wounds, notify the police, and discharge them back to their reality—a reality that is much different from ours.

Crap! Next, in comes a pregnant woman with a gunshot

wound in her head. She has no identification, and she was found in a ditch on the side of the highway. We call her Jane Doe. She appears to be close to full term.

"Goldie, page obstetrics stat," orders Dr. Andrews. CPR is in progress. The obstetrics' team arrives.

Max raises his hands and says, "Stop CPR. Time of the mother's death is 2:10 a.m. That leaves us only four minutes to try to save the baby."

The OB doctor performs an emergency cesarean section. Sadly, the baby could not be saved, and it is pronounced dead at 2:14 a.m. By the way, the tiny crack pipe that was later found sticking out of Jane Doe's vagina was saved. I think, *Son of a bitch, go figure!*

There is no time for emotions. I have a possible stroke patient due to arrive any minute. The stroke team is standing by. A sixty-nine-year-old woman awakened and told her husband that she felt confused. Her speech was slurred. He called 911, and a squad is bringing her in.

Our medical center was recently designated as a stroke center. A twenty-four-hour on-call team of neurological, interdisciplinary professionals was formed.

Protocols are developed for timed restoration of blood flow in acutely occluded cerebral arteries. A CAT scan will rule out a cerebral bleed. We use exclusion and inclusion criteria to determine eligibility for thrombolytic therapy. Risks and benefits are discussed. There is currently a three-hour window from onset of symptoms to administration of thrombolytic. Prompt restoration of cerebral blood flow will preserve brain tissue. The biggest risk is hemorrhage.

The CAT scan does not show the patient, Mrs. Stein, as having a cerebral bleed. She is admitted, and she opts for thrombolytic reperfusion therapy. I am pleased to say that she ultimately has a good outcome.

I hear Dr. Metz call out, "All available staff to the trauma bay." Two people with gunshot wounds are coming in. Paramedics rush in pushing two gurneys. Several police officers follow them. The patient receiving CPR is a cop and is placed in trauma bay one. The other patient is being taken to trauma bay two.

The medics have removed the police officer's bulletproof vest and his shirt in order to provide CPR. I cut off the remaining bloody clothing while CPR continues. I pull off his shoes—a pair of steel-toed boat shoes.

I think, *Oh shit! Fuck! It's Officer Billy! He sustained a gunshot wound to the head. Oh no, he was shot by the patient in bay two.*

Several staff members are tearful (including me) as we frantically perform advanced cardiac life support, led by Dr. Andrews. I never heard so much swearing in my life.

Dr. Metz is running trauma in bay two. He says, "Staff, I need some help over here stat!"

No one wants to work on the son of a bitch who shot Billy. I force myself to go to bay two. Janette follows me. The bottom line is that we all took oaths to save lives— even the life of a stinking bastard.

He has a gunshot wound on his right shoulder. His right leg and left arm are handcuffed to the gurney as a police officer stands guard and we provide care. The patient is oriented but not talking to Dr. Metz or any of us. The cop tells us that the patient's name is Malcolm and that he has a record for selling heroin and assault with a deadly weapon.

We stabilize Malcolm (aka Scumbag, in my mind) and send him to the operating room. The police officer goes with the patient and us to the OR. "I'm not letting this prick out of my sight," he says. We leave them and head back to help treat Billy.

There is an eerie silence. Dr. Andrews places a hand on Janette's and my shoulders and quietly tells us, "Billy is dead."

I think, *Billy died, and the bastard who killed him lived. Why?* There is that mysterious nanosecond thing again between life and death. It's so surreal. I'm trying to hold back the tears.

The police are still here waiting for Billy's family to arrive. His wife needs to see Billy before he is taken to the coroner. I feel numb. I feel nauseated. We have to focus on the rest of the patients until our shift ends. We all agree that we are exhausted, are somewhat traumatized, and just need to go home. Thank goodness, I am off tomorrow.

8

I SLEPT ALL day. I am now wide awake, am still feeling sad, and am stressed from losing such a good cop while saving the killer. I change my focus and think about the new, handsome guy and his fabulous sailboat. That makes me feel better. I look out a hatch and see that his boat is gone from the dock. Damn, I wonder if he would have asked me to sail if I hadn't been secluded and wallowing in my grief.

There is a party tonight at Frank James's home. He is a resident physician who rotates through the ER. I think I'll phone a couple of the Hobags and see if they are going. "Hi, Lena, are you planning on going to Frank's party tonight?"

"Yes. I just got off the phone with Dana and was about to call you. We can pick you up at eight."

"Super. I'll be ready. Bye now."

"See you later."

The girls pick me up, and off we go to the party. We each bring a nice bottle of wine to give to Frank.

"Great minds think alike," Dana says and then laughs.

We all agree that getting out of the house beats lying in bed and feeling miserable over something we couldn't control. We all did the best we could.

Wow, the party is jumping. There's great music, good food, and a well-stocked bar. Half of the ER's staff and several medics are here. We are dancing and having a great time.

"All this wine, Frank, where is your bathroom?" I ask. He points to one down the hall and to one at the top of the stairs. I opt for the one down the hall. I pull my pants down and take a seat. All of a sudden, I see a huge snake rise up from the tub and poke its head out from behind the frosted-glass enclosure.

"Snaaaaaaake!" I scream like a banshee and run clumsily out of the bathroom with my pants still around my ankles. Blindly, I flee out the front door with three or four friends chasing after me. I trip on my pants and fall down.

Jason grabs me, and I scream, "Don't touch me!"

"You are safe," He says and holds me. He talks me down while Lena pulls up my pants. Who knew Frank has two huge pet snakes? Who knew he thought everyone liked snakes? Who knew I've had a phobia since a poisonous snake bit me when I was a kid? I am still shaking. Lena goes into the house to say goodbye for the two of us and ensures Frank that I am okay.

"Dave will take Dana home. Come on, Goldie. I'll drive you home."

"Thanks, Lena. Thanks, Jason. Oh shit, Lena, I have to face all these people at work after they saw my sorry naked ass streak through the house."

"Don't worry, Goldie, they see hundreds of bare asses every day. Ha ha. Chin up. After all, you are a Hobag." I laugh with her. Lena and I have a martini at the cabana bar and then say goodbye. I walk down the dock to my boat.

My two days off fly by, and it is 6:30 p.m. as I enter the ER. It is booming, and I jump right in. I am still embarrassed, but I display great dignity when I intermittently get a silly grin or a bare-ass comment from a peer. Sometimes it is hard to be me.

My first patient, Mr. Romano, has a blood pressure of 210/120. Yikes, that is stroke range. I start a dedicated IV line and hang a drug to lower his dangerously high blood pressure. I place him on a monitor, give Rob, who is his RN, the report, and then go to assist Myron Baum, who is suturing a struggling child's lip laceration. I check on Mr. Romano. His blood pressure is slowly decreasing. The stroke team is here and managing his care. I give him the thumbs up. His wife, who is sitting at his bedside, says, "Thank you for helping my husband."

"We are going to take good care of him, Mrs. Romano."

Next, we suture a laceration on teenage boy's left arm, which was caused by a jagged piece of glass. Just as I discharge him, EMS brings in a man who was involved in a minor auto accident. Once it is established that he has no neck injury, we suture the back of his head. His X-rays look good, and we apply a soft cervical collar because of his neck-pain complaint. He is going to be discharged soon.

Paramedics arrive with Miss Walker, who is a thirty-six-year-old woman and is believed to have overdosed on Tylenol. Lena and I set up so that we can place a tube through her nose into her stomach. This is so that we can perform a gastric lavage on this accidental overdose verses an alleged suicide attempt. We also start an IV and send blood work to the lab, which will include a toxicology screen. Lena stays with the patient. I walk out to the desk to sign off the doctor's orders and to call for a psychiatric consult.

Son of a bitch! I look into room eight. The door has been left open, and I see an obviously intoxicated man standing in the corner of the exam room urinating in the trash can. Oy! Now he is peeing on the wall behind the trash can.

"Hey Dave, you are needed in room eight," I say and then hurry past the door. This is proving to be an interesting night. I think, *Everyone brace yourselves.*

In comes a squad with a woman who is thrashing and shouting, "Let me out of here, you fuckers."

Thomas, a paramedic, tells her, "Calm down, Gale. We are trying to help you."

"Screw you," she says and spits at the medics. They can hardly contain her on the gurney. I hit the panic button, and help comes running. It takes nine people to hold her down and restrain her on the ER cart. We really don't like to restrain patients, but for her safety as well as ours, we have no choice. She will be closely monitored.

Gale continues to struggle and swear as we insert another IV and draw blood for lab work, which will include an alcohol-level and a toxicology screen. The staff is already taking bets on how high her alcohol level will be. The whites of her eyes are beet red. She has vomit down the front of her dress, and she is missing one of her high-heeled shoes. Eventually she falls asleep. We keep the IV fluids running.

A very obese woman with a gunshot wound in her abdomen is wheeled into one of the trauma bays. Dave starts to cut off her clothes. As he cuts off her girdle, a bullet fragment ejects from her belly and shoots across the room.

I think, *Shit, I never saw anything like this before! Thank God that it missed Dr. Andrews.*

Max pales for a moment and then yells out, "Damn!" He then continues to assess and treat the patient. I am so glad that I didn't faint. I retrieve the bullet fragment, place it into a labeled specimen container, and give it to the police. Hooray for my forensic training.

"I can't think of anything worse than getting shot with a secondhand bullet," I whisper to Dave, and we chuckle.

"Very funny," remarks Dr. Andrews as he gives us a dirty look.

Then it's back to business. I am asked to help in triage. A patient named Anthony, a college student, is brought in by one of his roommates. Anthony looks very uncomfortable and states, "I will only talk to the doctor."

He is placed into room ten. Back in triage, his friend tells me that Anthony was practicing something called auto-erotic asphyxiation. He further explains, "Tony placed a gerbil into a plastic baggy and inserted it up his rectum. He then masturbated as the gerbil thrashed while suffocating in the baggy."

"Really?"

"Yes. All that thrashing movement dramatically intensifies an orgasm. Unfortunately, today the baggy with the poor dead gerbil is stuck up his ass."

I inform Dr. Metz of the situation, and he takes Dr. Baum with him to see the patient. Dr. Metz is mentoring Dr. Baum on the use of an anoscope.

"Myron, if the baggy is greater than a six-inch insertion, we will have to send the patient to the OR. If it is less than six inches, it can be removed by us here in the ER."

It's a success. Dr. Baum is able to remove the baggy that has the dead gerbil in it. There is no way that I can look at that poor dead thing. Dave finishes the case.

Dr. Metz tells me there are other forms of auto-erotic asphyxiation. "A guy hangs himself as he starts to have an orgasm, but someone has to cut him down quickly." Dr. Metz adds, "I only saw one person brought into the ER who lived to tell about it." He tells me the trend is changing. "Candle removal is the more frequent thing we see, in women as well as in men. Oh yeah, also stuck soda bottles."

Dana chimes in, "One of the strangest ones was the young man with the lightbulb stuck up his ass. They had to pour plaster into his rectum so it wouldn't shatter when they pulled it out."

"Are you serious?" I ask.

"Yes, she is," states Jason.

"Oy! Damn full moon."

I hear a thud and run into room three. There is a woman sitting on the floor with a blood-pressure cuff around her neck. The piece of tubing that plugs into the wall-mounted BP machine is bobbling. It disconnected when she rolled off the cart.

"That is the most bogus suicide attempt that I ever saw," I say. I get her back on the cart. She has no apparent injuries, and she "don't want to talk about it." I get an order for a psych evaluation and place her on suicide precautions.

All of a sudden, a voice over the intercom shouts, "Hit the deck!" Everyone drops down and lies on the floor or crawls under a desk. The doors to the patients' rooms are closed. I think, *Son of a bitch!* I'm not sure what's going on out in the triage area. I suspect that it is a gun or guns.

"Everyone, please be quiet and stay down. Everything is under control," I whisper. It is scary not knowing what is happening. There is only one way out, and that is through triage.

Sure enough, after about ten minutes of taking shelter (while trying to keep an eye on our patients and their families and trying not to scream), security and the police apprehend a man. A voice on the intercom states that the situation has been secured.

Security informs us that the man entered the ER via the ambulance bay. He had a handgun and pointed it at one of the triage nurses, Carla. She yelled the warning over the intercom as she pushed the panic button. The man grabbed her and demanded that she take him to the place where we keep our drugs, otherwise, he would shoot her.

She started to go with him and then suddenly dropped to the ground like she had fainted. Police immediately jumped him and gained possession of his weapon. The man was cuffed, read his rights, and taken straight to jail. Patients and families are reassured that everything is all right and that there is no danger.

It is a miracle that neither Carla nor anyone else was shot. Carla is pale, and she is shaking. "I thought the gun that was pointed at my head was going to go off. I think I need to go home."

Max examines Carla, medicates her for anxiety, and discharges her with home-care instructions. Her husband is called, and he comes to drive her home. He is also asked to have Carla call human resources for counseling or stress management. He nods, thanks Dr. Andrews, and takes Carla home. Even this was too much for our hard-core Carla.

A similar event happened in another hospital's ER a year ago. One doctor, two nurses, and a police officer were shot. Two of them died from the gunshot wounds. It was so frightening. Thank goodness no one here was shot.

Incident reports are made. The media gets wind of the situation and shows up at the entrance to the ER. They are directed to speak only to a representative from the hospital's media department. She is on her way to the hospital. This event led to the installation of metal detectors in the ER. There's no time to freak out. We must get back to saving lives.

Morning is near. Gale, the woman who was drunk and was missing a shoe, calls me to her room. "Nurse, can you come here?"

"What can I do for you?"

She has sobered up, but she still looks like she is hurting.

I remove her restraints. Her alcohol level was three times the legal limit. "Nurse, I just started a new job. Can you call my employer and tell him that I am in the hospital and won't be in to work today? But please don't tell him why."

I tell her that we don't give out information and ask her for the phone number. Oh my! I look at her and say, "You work here, in this hospital?"

"I was hired two weeks ago. Oh, I hope I can go home soon."

I leave a message with the environmental services department as she requested and don't mention the hospital. It is between her and her boss. I hand off shift report and head for my car. Everyone is emotionally and physically exhausted, so we all head for our own homes.

As I am driving back to my boat, I think of Billy getting shot and dying in the ER. Then I think about the potential loss of life from tonight's gunman. There are so many things we can fix and so many things we can't fix. We just keep the adrenalin flowing.

As I walk down the dock, I see Drew walking toward me. "Good morning, Goldie. How long are you going to be working on the night shift?"

"One more shift, and then I am off for four days."

Drew escorts me to my boat and says, "I would like you to sail with me."

"Sounds like a plan, Captain Piers. Oh, by the way, on Saturday night, there is a costume ball at the clubhouse. I hope you will join us."

He gives me a hug and his signature kiss on my forehead. Then he says, "Only if I will be able to pick you out in the crowd."

"I think you will. See you there." I smile, say goodnight, and climb aboard my boat. Sleep sounds so good right now.

Sleeping during the day is not easy for me. I toss, turn, and wake up frequently. Inevitably, my alarm goes off when I reach the deep-sleep phase. Go figure. I shower, blow dry my hair, apply makeup, don my scrubs, eat a protein bar, and wash it down with my favorite cola. I get into my car to join the other Hobags at the ER.

As I am driving into the hospital's parking garage, I see the helicopter landing. The ER is packed. The helicopter team has just brought in a fifty-six-year-old man from a catastrophic auto accident. He has a severe brain injury. Dr. Vaughn and the nurses are trying frantically to save the man.

His driver's license notes that he is an organ donor. His wife arrives in the ER. I bring her to a private area and say, "Mrs. Carlyle, your husband is very critical, and we are doing everything we can, but he is not responding. Would you like me to take you into the trauma room?"

She is sobbing, and she states, "I just can't face it right now."

"I know this is difficult to talk about, but your husband's driver's license indicates that he is an organ donor. Are you aware of this?"

"Yes, we both believe in it."

Back in the trauma bay, Dr. Vaughn states that the patient is brain dead. She stops the resuscitation attempt for a few seconds to place the patient on a chest-compressor device to keep blood flowing until the possibility of organ donation is confirmed. Mandy, the respiratory therapist, continues to manually provide 100 percent oxygen.

Dr. Vaughn comes out to talk to the wife. "Mrs. Carlyle, I am sorry, but your husband obtained a severe head trauma. Despite all of our attempts, I have confirmed that he is brain dead. His driver's license indicates that he wishes to be an organ donor. We are keeping his heart pumping blood with a device that pushes on his chest as if CPR is being performed. If you wish to donate his organs, he will go to the surgical intensive care unit until the operating room and the organ donation representative are ready."

His wife looks at us with tearful eyes. "I will sign any consent forms. Can I see him now?" We then escort her into the trauma bay to be with her husband on his final journey.

9

RAPE IS A violent act against women, children, and men. Penetration may be vaginal, anal, or oral. It is often too terrible to talk about. There are many ways that rape presents in the ER, and all are documented as "alleged rape." It is up to a court of law to rule on the legitimacy of the act and the fate of any perpetrators.

Those of us who are trained to care for alleged rape patients provide one-on-one care until the evidence is obtained, secured, and turned over to the sex crime unit. The time of the procedure can range from three to six-plus hours depending on the type and severity. Here are some of the types that we receive in our ER:

- Acquaintance/date/partner rape
- Incest rape
- Diminished-capacity rape
- Blackmail rape
- Control rape
- Anger rape
- Hate rape
- Abduction with rape
- Group rape
- Gang rape
- Pedophile rape
- Rape with a gun, knife, and other foreign objects
- Rape with a beating/violence
- Rape with torture (This type is unimaginable, and it can stimulate nightmares)
- Rape and murder (Most of these don't make it to the ER)
- Delusional rape or perhaps fraudulent rape

God help me. I have seen them all. Documentation is crucial. It must be accurate, detailed, and objective. Many times, I have been subpoenaed to court to testify on an alleged rape case when I have been the nurse on record. The case may go to trial several years after the incident. Who can remember everything? I have to rely on my charting of the examination and evidence collection. I describe in detail everything I see that may be viewed as subjective so that I may be able to adequately answer objectively during cross-examination. My special training in conducting sexual assault examinations is a factor in obtaining justice for victims.

Do miracles happen? Does ESP (extrasensory perception) exist? EMS brings in a young woman who was raped and brutally beaten. Carl, the lead paramedic, tells me that the squad was driving down a winding boulevard when it spotted a car down in a ditch.

Carl holds my hand and tells me, "We called the police, and we all looked around, but we couldn't find the driver. We left the scene. As we were driving, my gut kept telling me to go back. The feeling was overwhelming, so I turned the ambulance around and went back to the scene."

"Wow, Carl, I am in awe."

"A tow truck was pulling the car out of the ditch. I told the cops about my feeling to continue the search. We spread out and conducted a wider search. I looked in this large drainage pipe and saw the bloody, bruised, nude body of a woman. I could barely hear her whisper, 'I knew you would come.' I yelled for the others to help me carefully remove her from the pipe, cover her with blankets, place her in spinal precautions, and get her into the ambulance. Now here we are."

"Unbelievable, Carl, you saved her life. Thank goodness you listened to your gut." Is it a miracle or is it ESP?

There are also many forms of abuse without allegations of rape. One example is Della. She has been coming to the ER every few months after her husband beats her up. She tells the police that she won't prosecute him. "I am afraid," she whispers to me. It is noted that each time she comes into the ER, the beatings appear to be more severe.

"Della, please let us help get you to a women's shelter."

"No," she replies as the tears stream down her face.

"He will find me, and it will be worse. He handles all the money, and I won't be able to support myself."

"Della, we have social workers who will help you. I am worried about your safety."

"I'll be okay. He just gets like this when he is drunk." That is all she would say.

"Della, it has to be your decision. We are here for you anytime that you change your mind." She is discharged and given a cab voucher to get home.

Later in the shift, I rush to trauma bay one. The medics bring in a woman with a steak knife in her right eye. Oh my God, it's Della! Della died.

There's no time to cry. More trauma patients come in. Thank goodness that it is the end of my shift. I am really looking forward to the next four days off.

10

I AM EXHAUSTED as I pull into the yacht club's parking lot. I have to get right to bed. I hope I can get a few hours of uninterrupted sleep. The costume ball is tonight at the clubhouse.

The alarm goes off. Wow, 4:00 p.m. sure came fast. I am excited as I get ready for the party. I don my costume. I'm dressed head to toe in black leather. I know it's very sexy.

I enter the clubhouse. It is lavishly decorated, the buffet is set, and the bar is packed. The band is playing. People dressed in incredible costumes are dancing. A group of my favorite fellow boaters shouts, "Welcome commodore."

"How did you know it was me?" I say and then burst out laughing. Denny, the bartender, hands me my favorite vodka martini. I feel a tap on my shoulder. I turn around.

It's Drew. I say, "So you recognized me," as I remove my mask. He gives me a smile and a kiss on my forehead. He too is dressed in black leather. What a coincidence. He takes my hand and leads me to the dance floor.

When we return to the bar, we socialize with other yacht-club members. Drew speaks softly and is an excellent conversationalist. We all agree that we have never seen so many terrific costumes.

"The judges are going to have a hard time picking out the winners who, by the way, will receive impressive monetary prizes. There are so many creative costumes," I comment.

The guy who wins is wearing a barrel with a round hole in the front and a sign that says, "Put in a nickel and pull out a pickle." Oh boy! Even though I did not win the costume contest, Drew invites me to go to his boat. I think I am the real winner of the night.

Drew takes my hand, and we walk out of the clubhouse. I stop and sit down on one of the poolside chairs. My feet hurt. I am wearing leather, thigh-high boots with spiked heels. "Drew, I have to remove these boots so I can walk down the dock."

"No problem," he says and then lifts up my right leg and slowly removes the boot. He then even more slowly, removes the left one. My heart is pounding as he hands me my boots, picks me up, and carries me to his boat. He sets me down onto a cockpit seat and then climbs aboard. Once on board, he pops open a bottle of champagne. We toast and sip the bubbly. It is wonderful, and I am flying high. What an evening. I think I'm in love. I know I'm in lust. The hot details will remain in my brain for now.

In the morning, Drew makes breakfast. "Goldie, spend your days off with me."

"Awesome. I just have to run to my boat and get a few things."

When I return, we go for a sail. What an incredible four days off. This is my new emergent sea stress relief. Tomorrow, I will return to my reality in the ER. Drew walks me to my boat, gives me a smile and a little kiss, and then returns to his boat. I get ready for bed, still smiling from ear to ear.

I hear an alarm. It is my clock awakening me from a deep sleep. I feel so happy. I am singing in the shower. Gee, I hope no one can hear me. I once took singing lessons, and I was told to save my money. I couldn't sing above middle C. I don my scrubs, have a cola and some toast, hop off the boat, and head down the dock to my car. I pass Drew's boat. There are no signs of life there. I can't wait to spend more time with him.

As I enter the ER, the place is jumping. It is the usual organized chaos. I hear Max say, "Hey Goldie, sorry I missed the party. How was it?" I tell him that it was incredible. "You look happy. You must have gotten laid," he says and then laughs.

"Emergent sea stress relief, Max," I say, grinning.

My morning is somewhat uneventful. I treat three cases of sexually transmitted diseases and two patients from minor car accidents, who require X-rays, sutures, and soft cervical collars. This is followed by a couple of diabetic emergencies, four chest pains, and a schizophrenic who has stopped taking his meds. I then care for several children with fevers and a few asthmatics. Life is good.

11

MY BLISSFUL MORNING is abruptly coming to an end. A strong voice is heard over the intercom, saying, "All available hands to the trauma bays stat. Awaiting two squads." Valerie, the secretary, is told to call the operating room and to have them standing by for a twelve-year-old with multiple stab wounds.

The first squad enters. Carl, the lead medic, is providing oxygen to an intubated boy who is covered in blood. All of his pressure dressings are now saturated as the bleeding continues. Traditional IV's could not be started, so intraosseous needles were placed in the tibia bones of his legs. Fluids are running with the aid of pressure bags to help move the fluids through the bone marrow. His blood pressure is difficult to obtain manually.

Dr. Andrews does a rapid assessment of his multiple stab wounds and reapplies the dressings. Carl assists the ER's personnel in transporting the child to the OR, where he will receive blood transfusions and undergo several surgeries.

The second squad enters. They have a male patient with a knife wound in his left shoulder, which is covered with a bloody dressing. The patient has a blank expression on his face. He is handcuffed and is accompanied by two police officers. George and another medic are wheeling him in on a gurney.

George reports, "This is the father of the male child whom you received a few minutes ago. In the frenzy of stabbing his son, he lacerated his own left shoulder. Our squad was called as backup, so I don't know everything that happened in that house. We moved really fast."

"Oh shit, he stabbed his own little son? That bastard," whispers Mae. Dr. Vaughn x-rays and then sutures the patient. He is being admitted to the psych unit with a 24-7 police guard.

Carl returns from the OR. He looks stressed. "What's wrong Carl?" I ask.

"We got a call to this house, and we were told that police would meet us there. When we arrived, there was a crowd gathered on the front lawn, and a police officer was moving them back. A bystander was saying that he heard screaming and pounded on the door. No one opened it, so he called 911.

"Two other officers motioned us to stand back, and they approached the front door. They knocked on the door, identified themselves, and issued a command to open the door. The door slowly opened, and a naked man was standing there with blood running down the front of his chest. He didn't speak.

"One officer stayed with him, and the other one went inside. We heard him shout, 'Get EMS in here quick!' We cautiously entered and saw him standing over the young boy we just brought in. There was blood everywhere. He was critical.

"While I was trying to secure an airway to assist his breathing, I looked up and saw a human head on top of the stove. I can't even tell you the other things I saw. This man killed his wife and three kids. Only this son survived."

"Oh my God, Carl, do you want to see Dr. Andrews?"

"No, I'll be all right. I just need a few minutes. I see all kinds of tragedies and life situations. At the end of the day, it's all about what goes on in our lives and how our lives appear to others."

"That's so true. I think we see it all in the ER, but you first responders see things that other people never will. Hang in there buddy."

I am called to triage and am asked to bring a sheet with me. A young woman literally just danced into the ER. She is singing and topless. She has a happy face painted on her right breast and a sad face painted on her left breast. I see Carl smiling. I'm sure that helped his solemn state of mind. We manage to wrap her in a sheet, take her vital signs, and place her in a private exam room. Dr. Vaughn sees her and orders a psych evaluation. The patient just keeps on singing. She obviously favors her right boob.

I think, *Oy! What planet am I on? Is it time to go home yet? No, I just got here.*

Carl and his partner, Robby, return with a twenty-eight-year-old male who says that he swallowed his toothbrush. How in the hell do you swallow a toothbrush? On our initial exam, he looks fine. There are no signs of any trauma to his throat. An X-ray is obtained, and there is no sign of a toothbrush in his esophagus or stomach. The patient wants to be transferred to the hospital where he normally goes for care. We grant his request, call a report, and transfer him to City Hospital.

Like always, we are busy, and it is rare that anyone has time to go to the cafeteria. So when Nurse Rachael is on duty, we grab a bite from her Crock-pot in the EMS room. Either way, it's another day of nibble when we can. The hospital provides nice boxed lunches. Unfortunately, they are only for the patients. You have to sign them out, otherwise, they would all be gone.

I still don't have time to go to the restroom. I'm too busy. I just hold it for twelve hours. I envision that we are all going to have bladder problems when we get older. That's enough bitching. I keep moving.

Triage is backed up. I go there to help Janette. A young woman brings in her four-year-old daughter. She has a fever of 104 degrees (Fahrenheit). She is coughing and using her accessory muscles to breathe. Her breath sounds are diminished, and she has a very low oxygen saturation. She is lethargic.

Her mom says, "She drank a cup of milk a few hours ago, and now she is very sick."

I highly suspect an aspirational pneumonia. I need to get her quickly triaged and to a treatment room, where she'll be put on high-flow oxygen. The physician will see her, order a chest X-ray (among many other treatments), and provide the definitive diagnosis. I ask the child's name. It sounds like the mother says, "Vahyinah." I ask her to spell it. "V-A-G-I-N-A." Then she pronounces it, "Vayinah."

I think, *Really? Are you kidding me? This poor child has enough to bear with her name. She doesn't need pneumonia too.* I take Vagina to the treatment room and send her mother to registration.

We get a call that City Hospital is sending our twenty-eight-year-old patient back. They report that they found the toothbrush, and the patient wants us to remove it here. The medics arrive. They laugh as they hand me an X-ray with a tube of toothpaste attached to it. Damn, the toothbrush is lodged up his ass on the X-ray. We prep him for the OR. The case of the missing toothbrush is solved.

A man enters the ER with his girlfriend, who is in a wheelchair. He hands me a teacup. In it, there is a piece of body tissue. He tells me he was having oral sex and states, "I bit off a piece of her, you know, and I put it in the cup. She didn't feel anything because she's paralyzed from the waist down."

I look in the cup and think, *One lip or two?* We prep her for an exam by Dr. Vaughn. Yep, he bit off a small piece of her labia, which cannot be reattached. Wow, he sure got carried away. This is a most unusual situation. I call out to Dave, "Hey Dave, go inform the man that is not how you eat pussy."

We are getting ridiculously busy. I will stay a little later than my shift to help. I assist with three cardiac arrests. We are adrenaline junkies. Bring on some more.

The man in room eight, who was screaming and holding his ear, has stopped screaming now that we have drowned and removed the cockroach from his ear. We see quite a bit of bugs in ears. We carefully look to insure that there are no other bugs on the patient.

My four hours of overtime are up. I'm pooped. I'm out of there.

12

IT IS THE 1980s. AIDS—What exactly is this disease that everyone is talking about more and more every day? It is now in epidemic proportions and is affecting not only homosexual men but also straight men and women. It can come from blood transfusions, dirty needles, having multiple sex partners, and transmission of (HIV) AIDS-induced viruses when exposed to blood, semen, and other body fluids.

The more we learn about the disease, the more frightening it has become. Because of the initial fear of the unknown, many of these patients are shunned by their families and friends. Many medical personnel are afraid to care for these patients. Their fear is that they might contract the disease. These patients are placed in strict isolation in the hospital.

In the emergency room, we don't know, unless they disclose their illness. We have to utilize great care when handling specimens and caring for wounds by frequently washing our hands and using personal protective wear. Blood testing cannot be done for HIV without special signed consent forms, and the results are only given to the physician.

I had a good friend who was an RN. I worked with him for years in intensive care. His name was Louie. He loved to sail with me, and he was good crew. Even better, I loved to go shopping with Louie. It would take me weeks to find clothes on my own that looked good on me. He would grab clothing off the rack, and I would immediately look fabulous in them. I'd ask, "Louie, how do you do that?

"You either have it or you don't, girl," he'd say and then laugh.

Then one day, he said, "Goldie, I have to cancel going to the mall tomorrow. I need a day to rest. I have been feeling tired, and I wake up at night sweaty and with a headache."

"Louie, this is so not like you. Promise me that you will call your doctor."

"Okay, I'll call in the morning for an appointment."

We had dinner and then went home. I had to work in the morning.

I got to the ER just as the medics brought in a thirty-year-old male who had passed out at home. His partner had called 911. He was wheeled back to the exam room. It was

Louie and his partner, TJ. Louie had a severe headache. His skin was covered with petechiae.

Blood was drawn, and imaging tests were completed. Dr. Andrews asked Louie for consent to draw blood for an HIV test. He told Louie that he had the signs of leukemia, which could be induced by AIDS viruses. "I want to admit you for bone-marrow and lymph-node biopsies."

Louie started to cry, and TJ looked shocked. Louis signed the consent form, had the blood drawn, was put into isolation, and was readied for transfer out of the ER.

"We love you, Louie," I said in disbelief. I thought, *This can't be happening.* Everyone in the ER was deeply concerned about Louie.

Two days into his admission, I went to see Louie. I put on my personal protective wear and entered the room.

He was in bed and started to cry. "I have leukemia and HIV. TJ and I have been together ten years. He had an affair two months ago. TJ is being tested as we speak. Goldie, I need a hug. Please hug me."

Initially, I was a little freaked out as I tried to process it all. Leukemia was horrible, but HIV was frightening. Two days earlier, everything had been fine, but now I was scared. I reached out my arms. He climbed off the bed, grabbed me, and held me tightly. He was crying on the shoulder of my protective gown. I hugged him back, wondering if tears carried the virus, but I couldn't think about that. I felt panicky and started to sing.

He released me, wiped his tears away, smiled, and started to sing along with me. I felt my fears lessen. I also felt good that he didn't feel totally alienated. He gave me the names of ER peers whom he wanted me to tell what was going on. Only Margo, Dana, Rob, and I were comfortable enough to visit Louie in the hospital.

We took turns having lunch with him and pretended that we were in other countries. We laughed, sang, and updated each other on Louie's condition. We tried to overlook our fears and to comfort our friend. We all were tested for HIV and were negative. We would have additional testing at six months and at one year. Many of the ER staff members had a yearly test done just to be safe for themselves and their families.

Louie's prognosis was poor. TJ came and spent the night with him. Louie asked for leave from the hospital so that he could sail on my boat. He was weak and in isolation garb as we helped him onto the boat. He had a wonderful time as he sang and steered the boat. After two hours, we returned to the yacht club. Then we got him back to the hospital. He was so happy.

I went back to my boat and got ready for bed. My phone rang. It was 5 a.m. It was TJ. "Goldie, please come to the hospital. Louie took a turn for the worse."

"I'll be right there."

I gowned up and entered the room. Everyone in the room was in tears. TJ grabbed my hand and said, "Louie died." I walked to the bed, reached for his hand, and sang him a song. I said goodbye and left the room with tears in my eyes. There was a private service for Louie.

13

THE EMERGENCY ROOM is expanding. It is adding four more trauma bays, four additional critical rooms, and office space on a second level. There is a lot of construction going on. Some of the existing rooms are temporarily walled off and have a door for the workers so that they can work and the patients will not see them.

You can't see them, but you can hear them hammering, sawing, and drilling. Outside and adjacent to the ambulance bay, there is a lot of heavy equipment, including a small crane. At 7 a.m., the crews arrive and begin their work.

EMS brings in a patient who has a gunshot wound in the head. I direct them to trauma bay two. As they run by me, one of them yells, "Go look at the crane stat."

"What?" I say, run to the ambulance bay, and look up at

the crane. "Son of a bitch!" I say as I see a woman climbing up the little lattice boom, truss, crane, or whatever the hell you call it. I hear her mumbling and sobbing as tears flow down her cheeks and she struggles to ascend each level.

I yell through the bay door, "Carla, get security, a doctor, police, and fire stat! We have an emergency out here." Carla runs to the door, looks up at the woman, and then runs to make her calls. I gaze up at the woman and say, "Hello, I'm Goldie. Please talk to me. I want to help you. What's your name?"

"Fuck you! Fuck everyone! Go away!" she says and continues to clumsily work her way up the crane.

Carla yells, "Help is on the way."

Dr. Leo Williams runs out, and I point to the woman on the crane. Security is busy clearing the area of the people who have been accumulating to view the situation.

"Ma'am, I am Dr. Williams. Please talk to me. What's your name?"

"Go away. I want to die. Go away."

"I'm coming up so we can talk. Please let me help you." Leo starts to slowly climb up the crane as he continues to calmly talk to her. "Call me Leo. Who are you?"

"M-M-M-M-Michele. I'm Michele."

As I watch, I am speechless. I think, *Please don't let me pee my pants.*

Security approaches and tells us that police officers and firefighters should be arriving at any minute. The other staff members in the ER are busy, but they poke their heads out as often as they can to check out the situation.

I call to Leo, "Dr. Williams, please come down."

The police officers who came for the gunshot patient step out of their cruiser and ask, "What's going on here?"

I look at them with wide eyes and say, "That woman is threatening to jump. Dr. Williams is getting close to the woman to try to keep her from committing suicide. Her name is Michele."

The police officer looks at the woman and yells, "Michele, this is Officer Rocco. We are here to help you."

"No, I want to jump."

"Dr. Williams, please come down."

Leo shakes his head, indicating that his answer is no. Dr. Williams is now very close to the woman and says, "Michele, please take my hand. I don't want to fall. I care about you and want to help you. Please take my hand, and we can go down together. Give me a chance to talk with you—to help you."

The crowd of spectators continues to grow. Security guards and police officers are busy keeping them behind their defined lines.

Leo carefully reaches his hand toward her. She lets go with one hand, leans back, and looks at the ground. I hear gasping from the people, including me. I am holding my breath and praying. I think, *Please don't fall. Please don't jump and pull Doc with you.*

I don't know what he says to her next, but she leans forward and grasps his hand. He moves closer to her and tightly puts his arm around her. She is shaking and sobbing loudly as she buries her head in his shoulder. The firefighters arrive, and Officer Rocco apprises them of the situation.

Officer Rocco calmly tells Leo that the firefighters will hoist up an apparatus for a safer descent. The aerial basket is raised, and the firefighters assist Leo as he seamlessly guides Michele into the basket. The firefighters then lower them to the ground and to safety. The crowd cheers. Michele is shaking, and she has her arms around Dr. Williams, who is wet with sweat.

He and a firefighter escort Michele to a private room. She is placed on suicide precautions. Lena will stay in the room with her, and a social worker is assigned to assist her. Dr. Williams stays and talks with Michele until the psychiatrist arrives, evaluates her, and admits her.

I thank the security guards, the police officers, and the firefighters. None of us understands why Dr. Williams climbed that crane. It was so dangerous. But he got her to safety and admitted to the psych unit for much-needed care.

The police officers and the firefighters make out their reports. The firefighters leave, and Officer Rocco goes to check on the gunshot patient.

I walk up to Leo and say, "Are you crazy? While climbing up there, you could have died."

"I don't know why, Goldie. Damn it, I felt I had to or she would have jumped."

I give him a hug and say, "I am really proud of you. You saved her life. Want to join us after work at the bar? We can talk more about it then."

"You bet. Don't leave here without me." He gives me a hug, and we go back to work.

A young woman walks in. She is crying and is carrying a small baby. I take the infant from her. I think, *Shit, this baby is dead.* I start CPR and call out to Rachael, "Call a ped code and take care of the mom." Several staff members come to assist me, even though we suspect the infant has been dead for a while.

When the pediatric-code team members arrive, they take over the resuscitation efforts and soon officially pronounce the infant as dead. The suspected diagnosis is sudden infant death syndrome. An autopsy will be conducted.

Sara, our social worker, is with the mother in a private room. The doctor tells the mother about the resuscitation. "I am sorry, but despite our attempts, we could not restart her heart. Your baby died a few minutes ago."

The woman just stares at him and says nothing. They hand her the infant to hold for one last time. Sara stays with them. They step out of the room to answer a page. When Sara returns, the mom and the baby are not there. She runs out of the room and asks, "Has anyone moved the patients from room eleven?"

I look up and spy the mother walking toward the exit door. She has a large bulge under her sweatshirt. I motion to the security guard as I scurry to cut in front of her. The security guard walks up behind her.

"Please come with us," I calmly say to her. She attempts to run. The guard takes hold of her arms, and I support the bulge under her sweatshirt. I then carefully remove the dead infant, which she was attempting to take home. She is sobbing, and she is escorted back to room eleven. A psych consult is called. She then is allowed to hold her baby with constant supervision and until she is admitted. Then the infant is transported to the morgue.

Unfortunately, the patient with the gunshot wound died, and he is being transported to the morgue. There is no time to learn any details.

As I return to the triage area, I hear shouting coming from the women's restroom, which is located in the ER's waiting room. Our male security guard asks me to go into the bathroom and assess the situation. He instructs me to keep the door open. He then stands by the open door so that he can quickly enter if needed. I think, *Why do I feel like a sacrificial lamb?*

Three women are yelling and swearing at each other. There appears to be no one else in the restroom.

I say, "Ladies, please lower your voices. You are in a hospital."

One of them turns, looks at me, and shouts, "Who you calling a lady, you fuckin' blond bitch?"

There is that name again. I raise my voice, saying, "Enough! Get the heck out of here or I'll have you arrested. Out!"

Security steps in and herds them toward the exit. They continue to yell at each other as they pass the onlookers in the waiting room and all the way out of the building. Thank goodness, they were all mouth and no action. Now it's back to saving lives.

The paramedics bring in a fifty-year-old male in full cardiac arrest. CPR is in progress. He has been shocked twice and given a dose of epinephrine intravenously. He has no history of events that led up to the cardiac arrest.

After thirty minutes of advanced life support, Dr. Metz asks, "Is anyone uncomfortable stopping CPR?" No one objects, so CPR is stopped, and Dr. Metz states the time of death.

There are no known family members to call, so the patient will be a coroner's case. As we begin to prepare him to go to the morgue, he sits up, opens his eyes, and says, "I'm back." Then he falls back on the cart into the unzipped body bag and closes his eyes.

"What the hell just happened?" cries Lena. Everyone is swearing and in disbelief of what we just saw and heard.

"Metz, get back in here stat," yells Janet. We check for vital signs. He is not responsive, and he is not breathing. He has no pulse or blood pressure. He has a flat line in all EKG leads when we place him back on the cardiac monitor.

"What the fuck? No one will believe this," I say and look at Janet.

Janet asks, "How are we going to chart this?"

"It's insane," Lena blurts out. "It's like a horror movie." She is laughing and crying at the same time.

Jason Metz looks at our freaked-out faces and tells us to document what we saw and heard. We are instructed to watch the patient for ten more minutes before we finish prepping him so that someone from the morgue or the coroner can pick him up—whoever comes first.

One broken leg, two asthmatics, one bloody lip, two kids with fevers, and then it's the end of the shift from hell. We give report, call Leo, and head for our corner bar, where we will ease some of our much-earned tension. Our decompression session awaits us.

We order our first drink and raise our glasses to Leo. Janet stands up to deliver the toast. "Leo, you scared the shit out of us. I don't know if you are brave or just plain stupid. Anyway, here's to our hero who climbed the crane and saved the woman."

We all toast him and share our feelings. We then focus

on Jason and the dead guy who sat up, spoke, and died again.

Dave delivers another toast. "Here's to Metz and his team. Here's to whatever. It is so freakish that no one will believe it anyway. Here's to no nightmares."

We all raise our glasses to Jason and say, "Here, here! Another round please."

We continue to talk and share our frustrations. We also laugh a lot. I can't keep up with these guys. They are on their third drinks. I am still sipping my first one. If I had three drinks, I would puke.

Dave jumps up on the table holding a pitcher of beer on top of his head. Lena is trying to get him to sit down before we are thrown out. Lucky for us, we always get the side room where there are no other customers.

Janet and Leo slip out together. *That's good therapy*, I think and then chuckle. I don't think I am imagining it, but Janet seems to slip out a lot. Oh well. After all, she was the original Hobag.

I excuse myself and leave while I can still drive safely. I have work tomorrow. Then I have five days off. I am looking forward to my emergent sea stress relief with Drew.

14

THE ALARM CLOCK rings. It is 5:30 a.m. I get out of bed and get ready to leave for the emergency room. This is my last day until my mini vacation. Life is good.

As I pull up to the hospital, I notice that there are a lot of cars in the ER's parking lot for this time of the day. I enter and take report from Rachael, who was the charge nurse on the night shift.

She says, "We had six major traumas that expired. There were gunshots, stabbings, beatings, and vehicle accidents, to name a few. It was like a MASH unit in a war zone. The morgue is full, and we had to place a body in the conference room while waiting for the coroner's office to pick it up."

Suddenly, we hear a man scream. Then we see a man,

who is wearing a hard hat, run out of the boarded-up area where the new trauma bays are being constructed. He is one of the workers and is intercepted by our security guard and Dick, an RN on last night's shift. They escort the worker to the security area to calm him down and to talk to him. They also temporarily block the entrance into the construction area. The other workers are waiting outside, and they are unsure of what is happening.

"Damn it! Shit!" says Rachael. "Goldie, we've been so busy that I just remembered we put the last dead body in the construction area last night. We had nowhere else to put him. We had planned to move him out when the coroner's people came to pick up the bodies before the workers arrived. Fuck!"

Gee, I'm glad I didn't work last night, I think.

The worker calms down. He and his coworkers are informed of the incident by a very embarrassed Rachael. The coworkers are teasing the poor guy, telling him that he "screamed like a little girl." They are laughing as he makes the others go first into the boarded-up construction area. The corpse was already moved to the only space available: the delivery area. A half an hour later, the men from the coroner's office pick up his body, along with the body in the conference room.

I am introduced to Dick. He is a long-standing ER nurse who has just returned from military duty. He grabs my boob and honks it like a horn. "Nice to meet you, Goldie."

I blow on his bald head. "Here's your blow job. Don't ever touch me again."

He laughs, salutes me, and then he walks away.

Rachael looks at me and says, "You'll learn to love him. He's really a great guy and a great nurse."

The night shift leaves except for Dick. He is going to stay and to help until 11 a.m. He truly is a highly skilled ER nurse.

Crap! We just received a call that EMS is bringing in an apparent overdose victim named Wayne. CPR is in progress. We just moved a patient to the operating room and then cleaned bay four, so we can move him in there. Dr. Donald Penske, a new resident physician rotating through the ER, leads the case.

The waiting room is crowded. Many members of Wayne's family are arriving. I take his grandmother, two brothers, and their wives into the social worker's office. I say, "CPR is still being performed. The doctor is working very hard to try to restart Wayne's heart."

Dr. Penske enters the room and introduces himself to the family. Then he says, "We did everything we could, but we were unable to revive Wayne. Wayne died a few minutes ago."

A sweet little old lady screams, picks up her cane, and strikes Dr. Penske across his face with it. Blood runs down his chin. I grab hold of her cane to prevent her from whacking him again. She tries to free the cane from my grip. One of the sons lunges toward the injured doctor, who flees into the bathroom and locks the door.

I let go of the cane, slip out of the office, and hit the nearest panic button. There is yelling, chaos, and banging on the bathroom door. Police officers and security guards rush in, restrain the family, and move them into the police room.

Dr. Georgius enters the bathroom and examines Dr. Penske after cautiously opening the door. He needs stitches in his lip, has a broken front tooth, and major bruising on his cheek. He gets an X-ray. He is awaiting the results to rule out a fractured facial bone. He opts not to prosecute the grieving old lady.

Carla walks in and whispers, "Good news, Goldfish, the morgue is now empty." Then she gets Wayne's body ready for transport to the morgue. Grieving family members are escorted out to their cars. Wow, this is the first time I have seen someone get violent while grieving a death, especially a cute little old lady.

"Hi, Max."

"Hi, Goldie."

I think, *Oh good, Dr. Andrews is working with us today.*

EMS rolls in with an elderly man who was found unconscious in a parking lot. I go to help and hear Lena singing some song about a mystery of life she found while she gazes down at the patient's penis. Oh my, he has the largest penis I have ever seen.

"Wow, I can see why you are singing, but can you keep your volume down?" I say.

Dr. Andrews does a double take and then continues giving his orders. "Dick, put a urinary catheter in this patient."

"Whoa, Max, I don't know if we have one long enough." He shakes his head as he walks out of the room.

Lena whispers in my ear, "He's probably jealous. They sure named him Dick appropriately." We chuckle.

The patient is stabilized. IV's are infusing, labs are

pending, he is intubated and being manually ventilated, X-rays and scans are completed, and oh yeah, the penis catheter barely fit but is secure. The patient is ready for transport to the ICU.

Police have identified the patient, and his daughter arrives in the ER. Yikes! This patient is the father of one of our night staffers. Dick consoles our peer before he goes off shift.

We treat an unconscious sixty-year-old female in a diabetic coma and get her transferred to the medical intensive care unit. Things are moving along normally.

Max declares, "I'm hungry. I think we have a few minutes to eat. Do you smell food cooking?"

"Sure do. Rachael left us mac and cheese in the EMT room," I tell him. One of the medics warmed it up, and everyone is grabbing lunch on the go.

I barely get my mac and cheese down when we are called to the trauma bay. Two young men are brought in from an automobile accident. EMS has them immobilized. We maintain their spinal precautions as we move them onto our carts, cut off their clothes, and conduct a head-to-toe assessment.

Both patients are awake and alert. The driver has a fractured right leg and a dislocated right shoulder. Orthopedics is looking at the X-rays. The passenger has a bloody nose from the airbag's deployment. He is complaining of a headache and generalized muscle pain. The neck and spinal cord on both patients appear normal. Max is going to admit them both.

More vehicle-accident patients come in. It's a bride and a groom. They had an afternoon wedding, and they were driving to their new home. Their car was clipped by another car, which was running a red light. It was witnessed by their best man and maid of honor, who were in a car following them.

We always have to go through patient belongings and list them on their charts, along with two of our signatures. The cop who arrived with the ambulance hands me a box filled with wedding cards—filled with money. *Shit! That could be a lot of money*, I think. I ask Tina and Janette to complete the belongings form and hand them the box. They tell me that they love counting money. I ask the security guard to stand by as much as he can. Dave and I go with Dr. Andrews to care for the couple.

Dave works up a report on the groom, and I work up a report on the bride. After a head-to-toe exam, neither appears to have any serious or life-threatening injuries. Their labs and X-rays are all good. Their neck and spine exams are negative for injury. The groom complains of pain in both legs and in his left shoulder. The bride complains of neck pain. Max orders a soft cervical collar for the bride.

I go to get one and to check on the money situation. The security guard is at the doorway. Janette and Tina are sitting behind two gurneys with piles of money stacked up on the carts, and they are still counting.

"$10,000 so far, Goldie," states Janette. The best man is assisting by writing the amount of cash from each card, inside of each card.

I think, *That's a good idea.* I inform them that we will be discharging the patients in about a half an hour or after they have completed their count. *Wow, that's a lot of piles of money. I am sure it's going to help the bride and groom feel better,* I think.

I smell something burning. Oh, it is the firefighters in the triage area. They have a lingering odor of smoke from the burning building they have just left. They bring in a man with 30 percent of his body burned and a woman with smoke inhalation. I can't imagine doing their jobs. The thought of entering a burning building scares the hell out of me.

It is time to discharge the bride and groom with their $12,500. Now we can give report and go home.

15

ONE OF OUR Hobag nurses is working on her master's degree and has reduced her ER hours to per diem. She is beautiful and smart, and she has an incredible sense of humor. She is the perfect nurse. Many of the other nurses want to hate her but can't. The single doctors want to date her (a few married ones too). Her name is Barbie.

It is July, and the new resident doctors begin their practices with us in the ER. Four of these residents are getting a tour of the ER by Dr. Georgius.

"Wow, Hobags, check out the tall, dark, and handsome one with the blue eyes," says Janette. His name is Adrien Shariff. He came to the USA from Egypt as a child. He is a brilliant physician and a fun guy when he is outside of the ER. Six months into his practice, he takes a particular interest in Barbie. He thinks she is such a doll.

On days that Barbie isn't working, the nurses practically trip over each other to assist Adrien. I pass him in the hall.

"Hi, Goldie."

"Hi, Adrien."

He tells me that he loves being here and says, "The cases are so interesting."

"I just placed a patient in room four that you might find interesting."

Approximately five minutes later, he and Janette exit room four. Janette is wide eyed, and she says, "What the hell is he? A werewolf? He scared me."

Adrien looks at Janette and says, "If he didn't hurt Goldie, I didn't think he would hurt us. I have read about this condition but have never seen it. It's called hypertrichosis. It's an over production of hair all over the body. It can occur in any gender or age—even infants. Yes, they have been called werewolves because of their appearance. Don't worry, Janette, there is no full moon tonight." We all laugh. Adrien goes to talk with Dr. Georgius before proceeding with his care for this patient.

Janette walks up to me in triage and says, "Bitch, why didn't you warn me? I thought I have a lot of hair to shave on my legs." We laugh.

"Well, don't feel bad. I freaked out when I had to pluck a hair off my chin. So get over it," I say. As I walk away, I see Adrien and Dr. Georgius enter the room to care for the hypertrichosis patient. Yes, it is rare, but it does exist. I can't imagine living with that diagnosis.

Patients keep rolling into the ER. Suddenly, a garbage

truck speeds into the ambulance bay. The driver jumps out, yelling for help. Some of us run out to assist the driver. "There is someone in my truck's waste bin. When the dumpster was emptied into the truck, I heard a man scream. Then I heard a thud. Then I heard nothing," the driver says.

Adrien quickly gets into hazmat garb. He climbs up on the truck and lowers himself inside with the assistance of Dr. Metz, Dr. Andrews, and two firefighter paramedics, who have just arrived. They remove an emaciated, unconscious man, who is covered in garbage. The man has a weak pulse and slow labored breathing. He is placed on spinal precautions and is bagged with 100 percent oxygen. His legs and left arm are splinted.

They enter the ER through the hazmat entrance, cut off most of his clothing, cover him with a sheet, and change their protective coverings. They don't have time to run the patient through the shower. *Shit, I hope he doesn't have any bugs,* I think.

We sign him in as John Doe. He quickly gets assessed and treated. His scan shows that he has multiple fractures and a brain bleed. He is intubated and given 100 percent oxygen manually with a bag connected to his breathing tube. We escort him to the OR, and he is scheduled post-surgery for the ICU.

The police are attempting to identify John Doe. They suspect he is a homeless man who was asleep in the dumpster when it was lifted and its contents were discarded into the waste-removal truck. It was the second dumpster that the driver picked up today. The man awoke and screamed as he was dropped. Sadly, John Doe will probably die from his injuries within a couple of days.

Barbie meets us at the bar after work. We make jokes about smelling like garbage, even though everyone involved showered after John Doe went to the OR.

Max lifts his glass and says, "Here's to our hero, physician extraordinaire, Adrien Shariff." We all raise our glasses. Adrien gives Barbie a kiss, and we fill her in on his heroics.

Within a year, Adrien and Barbie get engaged. Soon thereafter, they have an extravagant wedding. Barbie completes her master's degree and works full time in the ER until she gets pregnant. They buy an estate, have twins, and are the perfect family. We have all been to many wonderful parties at their home.

Barbie returns to work per diem. One Friday afternoon as she is leaving her shift at 5 p.m., she tells us Hobags that she is taking the twins to her mom's so that Adrien and she can go away together for the weekend. "I am so excited. It's a surprise where he is taking me," she says.

"Wow, I can't wait to hear all about it when you return," Lena says with a smile. She blows a kiss our way and leaves the ER.

Monday morning, Barbie doesn't show up for work. Something is wrong. Attempts to reach her and Adrien are unsuccessful. Janette calls Barbie's mother. Her mother is frantic and crying. She tells Janette that she just got off the phone with the police. "Neither Adrien nor Barbie called or came to pick up the twins. I am so scared," she says. Janette says her goodbye, and they agreed to keep each other updated with any new information.

Later in the day, we learn that the police broke into their home and found Barbie dead. There were signs of trauma, and strangulation is suspected. The coroner will determine the actual cause of death. There was no sign of robbery. Only her wedding ring was missing from her finger.

I am in disbelief, as is the entire staff. Our dear friend and fellow Hobag is dead. I wonder, *Where is Adrien?* A search is being conducted for our missing doctor and friend. I think, *What is going on? He wouldn't hurt Barbie, would he?*

As the family has a private burial for Barbie, the search for Adrien continues. It is surreal. It has been several weeks, and Adrien has not been found. The search has been expanded to an international one. Family, friends, and ER peers are being questioned by the authorities. We are traumatized. Police suspect that he killed her, but why? There were no signs that anything was wrong between them.

I think, *Where did he go? What about his children and his medical practice? We thought we knew him so well.* Our hearts break for the twins and Barbie's parents.

As we continue to care for our patients, there is an indescribable feeling of loss in the ER. The mystery will remain unsolved. The pain lessens a little every day, but it never goes away.

16

THE HUMAN RESOURCE department is offering support to any employees who need assistance with their grief. But for most of us, it's another day in the ER, doing what we do best.

We receive a call that we are getting two patients from a carjacking. One male sustained a gunshot wound to his abdomen, and the other male has a gunshot wound in his right leg. Both men were removed from the car and brought in by EMS, with the police right behind them.

Dr. Metz is caring for the patient with the more serious abdominal wound. At the same time, a police officer is questioning this patient before he is transported to the OR. The police officer assumed that the two men in the car were friends. The man states that he fought with the hijacker over the gun, and the hijacker shot him in the belly.

"Did he then shoot your buddy in the leg?" the police officer asks.

"That's not my buddy. That's the hijacker who shot me, and he got shot in the struggle."

Dr. Metz looks at the police officer. "His vital signs are dropping. We have to take him to the OR now." The patient is quickly transported for his surgery.

We later get a call from the OR that the man has died due to complications to his vena cava. Dr. Metz, who overheard the conversation between the deceased patient and the police officer, has to sign a dying-declaration form because he witnessed the patient identifying the hijacker before he died. I learn something new every day.

It's time to check on Will, the patient in room seven. He sustained a gunshot wound to his left thigh. He attempted to rob a man who turned out to be an off-duty cop. The cop pulled out his gun and shot Will in the leg as he tried to run away. He is sitting on the cart reading what looks like a Bible.

"So, Will, what have you learned by reading the Bible?"

He looks me in the eye and states, "Thou shalt not steal." He smiles and continues to read.

"Your room will be ready in about a half an hour. Then we'll get you admitted," I say. He nods, and I exit the room. Do I think Will learned his lesson? Probably not.

Suddenly, Tina grabs my arm and says, "Goldie, you won't believe this."

"Believe what?"

"The guy in room eleven, he has a tattooed penis." Tina

goes on to tell me that Rob asked her to bring a urinary catheter to room eleven. She stayed to assist Rob with the insertion of the catheter into the patient's penis, which appeared to have a tattoo of a dollar bill. The patient got an erection, and more zeros appeared. The dollar bill grew to be a one hundred dollar bill! "I swear that I'm not making this up. I think my eyes fell out of my head, and Rob told me to close my mouth."

I couldn't help but laugh. "Wow, Tina, that tattoo must have really hurt. Think of the planning and the artistic creation to get it to increase in value. I wonder how much it cost." I think, *Hmm, I wonder how I can get in there and see it.* Unfortunately, I never do.

I smell smoke, and the smell is getting stronger. Two firefighters come around the corner escorting Dana, who is pushing a gurney with another firefighter sitting on it and holding something covered in his lap. He looks very stressed. His name is Fred.

During a house fire, the handle of Fred's pickax fell off. Back at the station, he told his fellow firefighters that he had a new handle. He laughed hysterically, opened his fire suit, and stuck his penis through the hole in the ax's head. Everyone was wild with laughter and joking. I thought we ER people had a weird sense of humor and strange stress-relief tactics.

Then things changed. He got an erection, and he couldn't get his penis out of the ax. Fred started to panic, and the laughter abruptly ended. They padded the ax's head so that it wouldn't cut into him as he held it in place.

He is rushed into a treatment room. Dr. Metz examines him. He says that Fred's circulation is being cut off. Dr.

Metz immediately calls Dr. Lester, the head of urology. Fred is prepped for the OR, where Dr. Lester and someone from maintenance and engineering is waiting for him.

I am pleased to report that they successfully remove the axe and that his penis will be as good as new after a recovery period. I am sure that his peers are never going to let him forget this.

EMS rushes a patient into trauma bay one. "He accidently cut off part of his penis with an oscillating saw," the medic tells me. The other medic hands me a small basin with the severed half of the penis in a plastic bag on a bed of ice. His clothes were cut off by the medics, and he has a large dressing in place. He has an IV, he has been given pain medication, but he is still moaning loudly.

Janette looks at me and says, "Bet he won't be sawing anytime soon. He smells like alcohol. Do you think that had anything to do with this?" She draws blood and adds an alcohol level and a toxicology screen to his blood-work request.

Dr. Metz calls Dr. Lester, who is just leaving the OR. He scrubs and successfully reattaches the penis. He tells Dr. Metz that there is a good chance this patient will regain full function.

Lena walks out of room eight and says, "What is with the tattooed penises? I just assisted with inserting a catheter into a penis with a snake tattoo. Goldie, I'm glad you didn't have to grab that snake." She walks away, laughing hysterically.

I'm glad too. I'd run away and become hysterical, I think.

I assist Dr. Andrews with a man who has a history of

erectile dysfunction. He was trying to get a climax, and he inserted a cotton swab into his penis. "It's stuck. Please help me get it out, and please don't tell my wife," the man says.

Dr. Andrews removes it and assures him that we won't tell his wife. The doc and I leave the room shaking our heads. What will we see next? "What is this, National Penis Day?" I say.

Oh boy, one of the patient's in the cardiac area just went into full arrest. I go to help. Thank goodness, it's not another penis. Lena and Dick alternate doing the chest compressions. Dr. Metz is running the code. Everything is being done, but the patient is not responding. Given the situation, I think the code runs longer than usual.

Later in the shift, I ask Jason Metz why he prolonged the resuscitation efforts. He laughs and says, "Did you see Tina doing chest compressions? She wasn't wearing a bra, and boy, those babies were bouncing. Besides, it didn't hurt the patient to conduct the CPR a little longer."

"Oh my God, Jason! Really?" I just shake my head as I leave the area.

Firefighter paramedics arrive with a man that they removed from a burning house. He is unconscious, is breathing, and has a pulse. He has an established IV and no visible burns, but he reeks of smoke. He is a well-built man, who looks to be in his thirties. He has no ID, so we list him as John Doe. We draw an arterial blood gas and then briefly step out of the room while a portable X-ray is obtained. I reenter the room and chart the intervention. I have my back to the patient.

All of a sudden, I feel an excruciating pain in the back

of my neck and honestly see three stars. There is a loud commotion behind me as I hold onto the counter so that I don't fall. John Doe was given Narcan to reverse the effects of opioids. It took away his high. He awoke, jumped off the gurney, struck me in the back of my neck, pulled out his IV, and ripped off his cardiac leads.

He is being wrestled back onto the gurney by other staff members who are in the room. The panic button has been pushed. Security and additional staff members enter and restrain him.

Dr. Vaughn escorts me to another area and orders an X-ray. My neck hurts, and they immobilize it for the procedure. The incident happened so fast from behind that I didn't see it coming, so I couldn't defend myself. I think, *So much for my having a black belt and being a former martial arts instructor.* This is not good for my ego.

The X-rays show a stable fracture in my C5 spinous process. Thank goodness, there is no severe cervical spine injury. I have increased pain with movement and a headache, but otherwise, I feel all right. An incident report is filled out, a soft cervical collar is applied, pain medicine is given, instructions are set up with physical therapy, and then I am sent off duty for six weeks.

Several members of the ER staff visit me a couple days a week and keep me updated on the goings-on in the ER. I think, *Gee, I wish I was there.*

Speaking of visitors, here come Carl and Robby from EMS. "Hi guys," I say.

"Goldie, we needed safe harbor and immediately thought of you and your boat," Carl blurts out.

"You both look nervous. Why do you need safe harbor? What happened?"

"We got a call for a man shot in the street. We got there ahead of the cops, looked around, and checked for scene safety."

"There were no crowds, no gunshots heard, but only a bleeding man lying on the sidewalk in front of an alley," adds Robby.

Carl stammers, "We approached the patient, and then heard a male voice say, 'If I wanted him alive, I wouldn't have shot him.' We look up, and a man wearing a ski mask holding a gun pointed at us loudly states, 'You have five seconds to get out of here.' He then cocks his weapon."

"Fuck," says Robby. "We run to our truck and hear a shot. We jump in the truck, and Robby hits the gas pedal. I was too scared to even shit myself. We hear sirens in the distance, keep on driving, and here we are. Can I use your bathroom?"

"Of course. How frightening. I'm glad I could be here for you." I ask Carl, "Is there anything else I can do for you?"

"I'm okay. I'm just gonna call in and let them know what happened. You know I like excitement in my life, but this was over the top." We both laugh, and then they leave for their station.

My time off work is passing quickly. Drew is supportive and spends a lot of time with me. We have plenty of calm sails. Physical therapy is helping. I feel better every week, and then it happens: I am cleared to return to work. I promise myself that I will never turn my back on any patients or their family members again.

It's a wonderful feeling to get back to the ER, to jump on the roller coaster, and take the ride. I am greeted at the ER door with hugs and a welcome-back banner. It's back to life in a state of emergency.

Even though there's been trauma and drama, I have arrived. I am inducted into the elite ER nursing group. It is composed of Hobag RNs who have survived an injury in the ER and haven't quit. This group is known as the Certified Urban Nurse Trauma Specialists. I proudly accept my gift. My very own CUNTS mug (Confidentially, I am glad they have no T-shirt or baseball cap). Dr. Williams and Dr. Vaughn hurry by us.

Dr. Williams shouts out, "All available staff to the trauma bay. Incoming: victims of a violent attack. Hi, Goldfish."

Dr. Vaughn yells out, "Welcome back, Goldie."

We follow them into the trauma bay. Even though I love the adrenaline rush and saving lives, I was hoping that the emergency room would be uneventful today. It wasn't—shit!

Lightning Source UK Ltd.
Milton Keynes UK
UKHW040913031020
370944UK00003B/115